Marble City

Ari J. Kaufman

iUniverse, Inc.
New York   Bloomington

iUniverse books may be ordered through booksellers or by contacting:

iUniverse
1663 Liberty Drive
Bloomington, IN 47403
www.iuniverse.com
1-800-Authors (1-800-288-4677)

ISBN: 978-1-4401-9009-4 (sc)
ISBN: 978-1-4401-9010-0 (ebook)

Printed in the United States of America

iUniverse rev. date: 11/16/2009

To Maria, my guide and inspiration: past, present and future.

Special Acknowledgements

As always, I am deeply grateful to my mother, Toni Friedman, whose copy editing saved me from a number of embarrassing errors. Also, many thanks to Andrew Schwartz, Cheri Pogeler, Karl Scharnberg and Dr. Everett Nienhouse, all of whom read early drafts of this book and made essential suggestions and incisive comments that I believe bettered *Marble City* in the end.

1

Déjà vu is annoying, Isaac Hyde mused to himself as he turned his Nissan Altima toward the George Washington Bridge on a dreary November morning in Northeast New Jersey. It's even more annoying when it costs you $9 each time it reoccurs he thought while handing his would-be lunch money to the lady in the tool both. She looked as gloomy as the weather on all geographical sides of him, as he and thousands of others made their way to the New York side of the Hudson River---just as thousands have done, by various means, for hundreds of years.

Then traffic came to a standstill. As it always did. Déjà vu is boring too.

New York is a great city. Some call it the greatest in the world and many arguments back up that bold claim with merit. But just as Las Vegas seems great when you're carousing with friends and winning fistfuls of money, New York, like most major cities, looks better when you're there by choice, not day after day amongst the masses, for the proverbial grind. Isaac could attest to this assertion.

This thought passed through Isaac's head multiple times per week for the past decade. He wasn't the Willy Lohman of the 21st century by any means, but sometimes he did fade into morning dreams of his college days in bucolic upstate New York, Manhattan Saturday nights of yesteryear, or his childhood in the serene Maryland exurbs of Washington DC. Then, providentially, he'd wake up and hit the brakes just in time to avoid the ubiquitous Con Edison truck often in front of him on the 80 year-old double-decker bridge. Déjà vu all over again, as Yogi Berra once said.

The George Washington Bridge, which literally connects historic Fort Lee, New Jersey, to the Manhattan neighborhood aptly-called Washington Heights, carries roughly 300,000 vehicles per day. It is the fourth largest suspension bridge in the United States, connecting the nation's largest city with massive highways like I-95 and US 1. Fewer than three miles west, it anchors the beginning of Interstate 80 which eventually takes its guests 2,900 miles across America the Beautiful before depositing them in San Francisco's Embarcadero at the termination of the Bay Bridge. It is a vital bridge.

Though he had visited San Francisco numerous times and did not care for the city, on days like this, Isaac often considered doing a 180 and heading west, west and farther west.

But it was just a thought. Isaac Hyde had a wonderful family.

His wife of nearly 18 years, Ana, was the consummate loving, caring woman. He had made her acquaintance shortly after their respective college graduations. Their birthdays fell just two weeks apart in the "neutral year" (as the Hydes deemed it) of 1962. They were born after the family-oriented Eisenhower 50s and before the turbulent Kennedy/Johnson/Nixon 60s and early 70s. They had the good fortune of being too young to come of age during the counterculture era, and had been raised modestly and pleasantly in the mid 70s by loving families who sheltered them from the tumultuous Carter Administration, releasing them into the world as the optimism of Ronald Reagan overtook America in the 1980s.

But, though born just weeks apart and reared in families with similar values, their childhoods were also vastly different.

Isaac grew up in a middle class Jewish family in Gaithersburg, Maryland. Now considered a suburb of Washington DC, even 20 years ago, much less 30-40 when he came of age, it might have been the end of the world for the sophisticated folks who commute along the beltway from the Maryland suburbs of Bethesda, Potomac and Rockville to The Nation's Capital.

Physically, Gaithersburg lies a tick under 30 miles from the White House. However, as it also sits half a dozen miles from the erstwhile distant exurb of Rockville, few folks considered it part of DC's metropolitan area. On many days, it takes drivers an hour or more to make their way into Washington.

Isaac's parents, originally from the New York City area, relocated to Gaithersburg in the late 1950s, more than two decades before New Urbanism became en vogue. They thus saw Gaithersburg go from a quaint, rural hamlet of roughly 15,000 denizens with a genuine small town feel to Maryland's third largest city with its current total of nearly 60,000.

When David Hyde headed southwest from New York toward a small town in Maryland to become a writer for the town's new newspaper, *The Gaithersburg Gazette*, his family considered him crazy. He'd have thought you were crazy if you told him that by the time his grandchildren were born (in 1993 and 1997), the land he bought his first house on---then used by the National Geographic Society for potential wildlife sanctuary---would have been transformed, beginning with New Urbanism in the early 80s, into "Montgomery Village," and a few years later, "Kentlands." Both were pleasant, concrete suburban jungles to the extreme.

What occurred? Well, as more and more people made money, especially in the 80s, they gobbled up the large estates closest to D.C. and forced the more middle class to move farther north and west. When tech companies, non-existent 30 years ago, like IBM and Lockheed Martin, set up offices in Montgomery County's County Seat, Gaithersburg grew. When century-old organizations like the National Institute of Standards and Technology and food service giant, Sodexho, moved their headquarters to the town, Gaithersburg boomed.

The town that began in the mid-1870s with a small Victorian B & O Railroad Station now boasts of having more than one-third of its population foreign-born. And though many residents hop on the Washington Metro's Red Line at its western terminus in Gaithersburg, many still work locally. Today, the city's median family income is nearly $70,000 annually.

By the mid-90s, when David Hyde retired after nearly four decades at *The Gazette,* Isaac realized that his dad's half-hearted expressions like, "We're the only middle class folks left here," really meant his parents could not afford suburban Maryland's cost of living any longer. The Mercedes-driving soccer moms, once assumed reserved for Chevy Chase, Glen Echo and other parts of southeastern Montgomery County just outside The District, had overrun the Hyde's once-quaint hamlet. There were 17 elementary schools, nine middle and five public high schools in the Gaithersburg area as of 2007. In 1957, there was but one high school.

One night, as David was perusing the city newsletter looking for senior associations to join, he came across an excerpt about the town's history.

He recalled many of the events fondly, especially as he had written about many of these occurrences. At the closing though, it read:

"Gaithersburg has undergone significant changes in recent years. The City is now an urban area and a suburb of Washington, D.C. It has become a major regional location for high-technology companies while commercial agriculture is close to non-existent. The rolling fields of wheat are now roads, housing developments and commercial enterprises...In the 21st century Gaithersburg continues to grow while retaining many of the qualities of a small town that cherishes its rich, diverse heritage."

The Hydes were both a few years past their 60th birthdays and well under ten percent of Gaithersburg's population was over 60. Gaithersburg, Maryland, was not only unrecognizable to the Hydes; it was no longer a place they desired to reside, much less a place to retire.

So it came to pass that David and Sarah Hyde moved to Surprise, Arizona, a similarly-booming, yet more affordable, mature and warm suburb, just northwest of Phoenix in 1997. This was the same year Isaac and Ana welcomed their second child, Ross, into the world.

The Mendez family originally hailed from Monterrey, Mexico. The country to our immediate south has it stereotypes, but Monterrey, its third most-populated city, has not only the highest Gross Domestic Product per capita in Mexico, but in all of Latin America. Sitting at nearly 2,000 feet above sea level, Ana's family always described it as very cosmopolitan and after his first visit just after their engagement, Isaac agreed, as he was taken on a whirlwind tour of this inland metropolis of nearly four million people.

Ana, however, never lived in Mexico. Her parents immigrated all the way up America's interior---nearly 1600 miles via station wagon---to Indiana around the same time Isaac's parents moved to Maryland. This was long before even one percent of the now 100,000 Latinos who now reside in central Indiana made similar treks, and decades before a population bomb occurred in the exurb of Noblesville. The histories of Noblesville and Gaithersburg were almost eerily similar, in terms of their distance to major cities (Indianapolis, as far as Indiana is concerned) and migration increase over the same time span. Isaac and Ana often talked about this, specifically when they first met. Noblesville had nearly 40,000 residents after a 2005 demographic update. In 2000, the city, like Gaithersburg, a county seat and just 27 miles from downtown Indianapolis, was home to fewer than 30,000 people.

Ana thankfully enjoyed a pleasant early childhood. "Thankfully," because Noblesville has a history of a KKK presence, though, like in the rest of the Hoosier State, nearly all of that died by the early 1930s. Still, rumors always existed of a recrudescence, and Noblesville is still a 96% Caucasian city, mainly Protestant.

Not that they had to "watch their back" as some had warned, but Ana's parents were always careful, especially after their first child, was born in 1962. This all considered, Mauricio and Carmen Mendez were fluent in English when they arrived. That helped matters a great deal, they always agreed. It seemed their new Hoosier neighbors greatly respected English-speaking, educated foreigners who were here to work, not to "abuse the system," as is often the case in immigrant havens like Miami, Los Angeles, New York City and parts of Texas.

Mauricio was a businessman by trade, but had difficulties establishing himself in America right away, so he taught Spanish at Ivy Tech Community College. Their two bedroom house was south of Noblesville's unique town square where the Hamilton County Courthouse sat. Carmen worked for the county's Historical Preservation Bureau, adjacent to the courthouse in Noblesville's town hall.

By the time Ana's brother, Kevin, was born in 1965, the family had moved west to a larger house between Noblesville and the city of Westfield. A slightly more rural community, Westfield sat just 21 miles due north of Indianapolis, and when Mauricio found a great job at Westfield High School teaching Spanish, History and coaching the school's baseball team in 1966, he jumped at the chance.

Mauricio Mendez had always heard teachers made paltry salaries, and his experiences at Ivy Tech, while giving him far more money than his parents ever earned as landscapers outside Monterrey, proved this---or so he thought.

Westfield Senior High School was at the very northwestern edge of the Hamilton County School District, which included the affluent Indianapolis suburbs of Carmel, Fishers and Geist. These areas paid better than nearly any school district in the Midwest, and with the lower cost of living in Indiana, Mauricio's take-home pay was quite good. And Carmen had been slowly climbing the city pay scale at her job, finding small "freelance" assignments along the way as well. Their life was on the fast track to the American Dream.

Ana graduated from Noblesville High School in 1980, the same year her father's baseball team at Westfield finally won the sectional championship. At Ana's graduation dinner, Mauricio joked that it was "bittersweet to "lose" his daughter but win the title."

Ana, who had played softball in high school along with amassing a high GPA and excellent SAT scores, was very happy for her dad, who had waited nearly 15 years for this accomplishment. He had played competitive baseball in college, and when not coaching or teaching, followed the sport closely, especially his beloved Cincinnati Reds, the closest team to Indianapolis and a multiple World Series title winning club in the 1970s.

While Mauricio continued as coach and teacher at Westfield, until his retirement at the very late (by teacher standards) age of 66, Carmen retired two years earlier. They both ended with incredible pensions, young enough to enjoy them. It was a good thing, too, as while Kevin had chosen four quick years at affordable Purdue University, then moved to Chicago to become an urban planner, Ana chose to attend graduate school and rack up some nice bills. As Mauricio put it, "I had to keep working to pay off those loans that added up quickly. I think her brain is worth nearly a million dollars."

Perhaps hyperbole therein, but Ana did "spend" five years at The University of Notre Dame in South Bend, Indiana, getting her degree in psychology. She spent one year living abroad and working as an apprentice to a social worker in Melbourne, Australia, between her sophomore and junior years. After that, Ana spent two more "long" years in New York City, earning her Masters in Clinical Psychology, where she then found employment at a local agency. Ana Mendez met Isaac Hyde a little more than a year later. They were both 27 years old.

Though a competent student with what his teachers called a "brilliant mind," Isaac's grades were never quite as good as they should have been. His SAT score of 1380, juxtaposed with his 3.2 GPA, supported that stance. Myriad reasons abound, as Isaac spent a lot of his spare time at the local batting cages working on his baseball swing. He was an all county player in both his junior and senior seasons at Gaithersburg High School, desperately looking for a scholarship to play college ball. His parents, though perturbed by his mediocre grades, understood the importance of baseball to Isaac.

David Hyde had been raised a die-hard New York Yankee fan, and he remained so for the 40 years he lived in Maryland, going to see the Bronx Bombers as often as he could when the team played in Baltimore. He had covered sports for a time at the *Gazette* in suburban

Maryland, but preferred news as far as writing went. David had always been perplexed that his only child never took to the Yanks, especially since Isaac first began watching baseball as the Yanks were entering a strong stretch in their history during the 1970s.

But if there was one other American League team as strong or stronger than the Yankees during that time, aside from the Oakland Athletics, it was the hometown Baltimore Orioles. Baltimore's Memorial Stadium was less than an hour indirectly northeast of the Hyde's house, and Isaac quickly made the Orioles his favorite team when they won the World Series in 1970 over the Cincinnati Reds. Baltimore followed with an AL pennant in 1971 and solid squads with legendary players for the next 12 years, culminating with another world title in 1983. Isaac was a fan for life by then, win or lose.

There were never any great father-son "showdowns," even though the Yankees and Orioles played in the same division, since the Yanks focused much of their animosity, as always, on the Boston Red Sox. The closest David and Isaac came to a rivalry series was in 1996 when the Orioles, after shocking the heavily-favored Cleveland Indians in the first round of the playoffs, took on the Yankees in the American League Championship Series and lost four games to one. David rubbed it in by inviting Isaac down to Baltimore for Game 5, with the Yanks already ahead three games to one and the series no longer in doubt. This was just weeks after David had retired and announced that he and Sarah were moving to Arizona. Isaac took off from work, drove the four hours down from New Jersey, and "enjoyed" the time at Camden Yards with his dad, even though his beloved Birds were clipped, much to David's delight.

At dinner after the game, Isaac and David both realized this was the first game they had attended together in more than a decade. It would be the last for nearly a decade as well, until a vacation brought Isaac's family to Arizona, where father and son took in an Arizona Diamondback game on a 100 degree June day. The roof was shut with the Astros in town, and needless to say, it just wasn't the same as watching baseball outdoors.

During the fall of 1979, with the Orioles in the midst of a horrible World Series collapse against the Pittsburgh Pirates, scholarship offers for Isaac's baseball ability were few and far between. Despite his grades and board scores still being considerably higher than most major sport athletes, Isaac was not a prototypical baseball player, at least physically. At five foot 11, 185 stocky pounds, he didn't appear particularly athletic. Further, as a pitcher, height was usually a prerequisite for standing out to college or pro scouts. What Isaac did have, as evidenced by two all-county selections, was good "stuff." He was also left-handed, a rarity in high school hurlers, much less professional and college pitchers. He threw in the upper 80s, had a solid curveball and experimented with a change-up that, when it worked, was literally unhittable.

Gaithersburg High School was not a baseball powerhouse, and never had been. Isaac pitched every other day his junior season, as he would his senior season. During his junior year, which mattered most as letters of intent to colleges had to be out by February of his senior year, long before the season even started back east, Isaac posted a 13-2 record with an ERA just under two. He struck out 104 batters in just 82 innings. But few scouts took notice.

And by the time he ended his senior season with similarly gaudy numbers (12-2, 2.05 ERA, 105 strikeouts in 86 innings), Isaac Hyde had only received baseball scholarship offers from three four year colleges: New York University, Bowie State University in Maryland, and a school called Clarkson College of Technology, somewhere way up in upstate New York.

At this point, his arm tired from so many innings worked in high school, and not really excited about any of those schools for various reasons, Isaac pondered college without baseball. He could instead attend a big-time "rah rah" school like University of Maryland, Ohio State, Penn State, Indiana or North Carolina, where he could study his favorite field of history, be around tens of thousands of people from all over the nation, be free from year-round baseball work-out obligations, and follow those schools' great athletic programs…like most collegians did.

It was not an easy decision. His mother and father were split. Dad wanted him to continue baseball at one of the schools offering a scholarship, while mom, quietly, preferred the other.

Isaac had no siblings, and his only long-term "relationship" in high school had been with a girl a year older, who was now at the University of Virginia (a "rah rah" school), thus consulting with her might have been futile as she'd be a tad biased. He also hadn't spoken to her in nearly a year.

Then one night, this long before the days of email, Isaac called this ex-girlfriend and left a voice mail. Two days later, just five days before letters of intent were due, she returned the call.

Amy Martin had been Isaac's first and last girlfriend to this point in his life. They dated from early in his sophomore year of high school until a few months before she graduated. Conveniently, she had been a softball player, though not stellar enough to get a college scholarship. She was, however, a brilliant writer, and had gone down to Charlottesville, Virginia to study English at what the locals call "Mr. Jefferson's school," due to the fact that our third president founded the colonial-style campus in 1819, some ten years after his time in office ended.

Aside from being a university with high academics, sitting roughly two hours south of Washington DC, UVA was also a public school, with over 20,000 students. It was, by virtue of being a long-time member of the Atlantic Coast Athletic Conference since 1953, a "rah rah" school. Students camped out before big basketball and football games, dressed in school colors for events (even wearing ties/ascots to football games in the preppy spirit of the Commonwealth), and had legendary athletes and political figures as alumni. This was a school that Isaac believed to be the quintessential type of college campus he had to consider versus the others with the baseball offers.

Isaac and Amy chatted amicably for about 45 minutes that cold winter night. After personal matters, he picked her brain for more information about life at UVA. Amy had both positive and negative opinions to share, which seemed refreshingly honest, since most first year collegians usually only mentioned the good: the parties, drinking, sports, casual relations, etc. Isaac was glad he made the call. After they hung up, he longed to see her again; to make a trip down to Charlottesville and visit her, as well as the campus. So he rang her back the following night, secured an invite (though Amy was not quite certain where he'd stay) and made plans to drive down that weekend as time was, literally, of the essence.

That weekend did not go as expected. Though Amy was cordial, she was distracted by her new life at college. She had this meeting here, that club there, this event over there and this friend she had to drive over here, etc. Further, the campus seemed, aside from the frigid temps, more like Florida State University or some party school after finals, than the esteemed University of Virginia in the middle of the second semester. Everyone seemed to be in some sort of post-Valentines Day funk or, depending upon how you looked at it, frenzy. It all seemed rather immature. And this was coming from the viewpoint of a high school senior. There will just too many rapacious kids drinking, making out, yelling across the quads and gossiping. It was redolent of high school, not an esteemed university. After fewer than 48 hours of hardly having time to catch up with Amy or see anything of the "real life" at

UVA, Isaac drove back up Highway 29, over the Potomac, around the Beltway and up I-270 to Gaithersburg. He was going to play baseball in college. Where that would be, however, needed to be ascertained quickly.

Given his limited options and time, the decision was made easily and quickly. Isaac Hyde did not want to live at home, and his parents were not keen on paying for room and board at Bowie State when it was only 35 miles away. And NYU, well, it was NYU. It had no campus, was extremely expensive for room and board, and baseball scholarships were not "full rides" like other sports. New York City was just too "hip" in a bad way, and that was that.

For a while, Isaac had trouble even recalling the name of the other school. Clarkson College was private, and in Potsdam, New York, with a renowned Tech School and hockey team. It had offered Isaac full tuition and 80% of room and board. It was fairly strong academically, and when the months were not between November and April, was a pleasant campus and town in which to reside. There was just one problem: Isaac and his parents had never bothered to visit the school. And with a blizzard on the way and the snow in extreme upstate New York not likely to clear for several weeks, this trip would not occur anytime soon.

Isaac capriciously signed his letter of intent to enroll as a student and play baseball at Clarkson College in Potsdam, NY, *sight unseen*. All Isaac knew was that the school had only 2,000 students and that this was not the same Potsdam that hosted the famous conference between Truman, Stalin and Churchill after V-E Day where the fate of Japan and the Atom Bomb was reviewed. No, sir, this was rural, hilly, serene Potsdam "Village," New York. And the good news was the spring visit the Hydes now planned would coincide with part of the very short baseball season in that part of America.

The Hyde family chose Mothers' Day Weekend 1980 for their 500 mile, eight hour sojourn from suburban Maryland to Potsdam, New York in David Hyde's 1978 Chevy Malibu. It was a particularly gorgeous weekend in upstate New York. All things considered, the terrain seemed a similar landscape to the scenery around northwestern Michigan, where the Hydes vacationed many summers during Isaac's youth. Though Potsdam's nearest body of water, the Saint Lawrence River, is not adjacent, ala the great lakes and bays of Michigan's peninsula, Potsdam's bucolic setting in the highlands just west of America's largest state park (Adirondack) reminded the family of that lovely area. It also seemed reminiscent of the Piedmont Region of Virginia that Isaac had seen near Charlottesville, as well as the rolling hills as you move west in Maryland from Gaithersburg..

The family "bonded" as best a family with an 18 year-old could. They ate great meals, stayed in a reasonably nice hotel, took a hike, and "took in" Clarkson's 9-0 thrashing of rival Union College at Snell Field on the edge of campus. It was Clarkson's 28th game of the season and they had just three left. Isaac was surprised that the season had been ongoing since late March, but was informed that the first ten games were played down in Florida during the school's spring break. That was typical among cold weather colleges.

Clarkson had lost nearly all those games versus Sunshine State competition and a scattered grouping of eastern and Midwestern schools also escaping the early spring chills. In fact, before this weekend, six of Clarkson's first seven home games had been postponed or cancelled due to rain, snow or simply cold weather. As of this May 8 victory, Clarkson had recorded only seven other wins to go with 21 losses. Isaac supposed the good news was that he'd likely be a strong contributor to the squad right away, even if they were losing often. The coach, with whom the Hyde family met later, assured Isaac of that---for what it was worth. While enjoying their time on campus, the Hydes all agreed this was the school for Isaac over the next four years.

And it was, as Isaac enjoyed moderate baseball success, especially in his freshman and junior seasons, before ceasing competition to concentrate on academics and his senior thesis during his final term. He was an all-Liberty Conference Selection his Junior year for the Golden Knights, when he was second in the conference in wins with eight and ERA of 2.39. By the time graduation rolled around in the spring of 1984, Isaac had carved out a nice little niche for himself in Clarkson lore. He had a stellar baseball career; had worked for the campus radio station as a basketball and hockey analyst; written a few commentaries praising Clarkson's Army ROTC program for the campus paper; met some nice friends, and most importantly, had maintained nearly a 3.5 GPA topped off by a senior history thesis on German settlements in Potsdam. In the thesis he had especially focused on those that formed a militia along the nearby Saint Lawrence River to defend America's borders during the War of 1812. It was a unique paper, highly regarded, and it spurred Isaac into a career in public history.

After graduation, Isaac returned to Maryland for a restful summer, then was able to catapult his talents into a job in a place none other than his father's former home of New York City. In a way, Isaac had come full circle. He was moving to the place his parents had left behind roughly 35 years prior. He had a congenial departure with his folks, and told his dad they'd meet up for Yankees-Orioles in the Bronx often. Isaac would still not cheer for the Pinstripers, though.

Born just three months apart in the same year, while Isaac and Ana's life paths brought both of them to New York City at the same time Ronald Reagan was re-elected, their careers had different beginnings. Isaac was employed full-time before his 23rd birthday, living the life of a Manhattan bachelor with roommates in a mid-town apartment and some disposable income. Ana was ensconced in the Morningside Heights area of Upper Manhattan, plugging along as a grad student at an Ivy League school.

Though this was the socio-politically "restful" period at Columbia University---between Vietnam and September 11, 2001---Ana was constantly on edge. She was earning a Masters in the very demanding field of Clinical Psychology; and, since she wanted a placid environment for her studies, she did not go out much. Her dad was helping her significantly with the bills, but she was watching every penny, had few friends, and certainly had no boyfriends. As it was, her program was 80% female.

Despite amassing more than adequate marks for her first semester, Ana was burned out in the depths of winter during her second semester. The only classmate that she could call more than a casual acquaintance was her roommate, Shari Lindsay, a native of Long Island. Though Shari seemed quiet and studious, Ana knew she came from quite a wealthy social circle in Glen Cove, New York, as well as from her years at Hofstra University, a nearby commuter school. Since this was graduate school, and thus, money cannot garner you admission nor success, Ana pondered how Shari was coping with the program. She was more than surprised to see Shari "setting the curve" so to speak in the small, nine-person Clinical Psychology Masters Program at CU.

This all told, Shari seemed more than safe and trustworthy to take Ana to a local hangout one cold February Saturday night.

Ana had not gone out much in college or high school. She simply did not enjoy watching people drink, carouse, and "act like fools" in her words. Some thought she was preachy for thinking and occasionally saying such, but Ana believed she was correct and was only trying to help. It just takes people time to look back and laugh at such scurrilous behavior, Ana often mused.

That night was much the same. Shari was flirting with guys, plastered within an hour, while Ana watched a basketball game on the TV high above the bar, watching the clock and waiting until an appropriate time for her to make the request of Shari that they leave. Ana didn't feel insecure or bored, just befuddled by people's antics at such an "advanced" age and state in their lives. She felt this kind of rebel rousing should have been eradicated from people's personas by the time they left college. Maybe Ana Mendez was wrong, but, confident as always, she doubted it.

Around midnight, with class nine hours later and a major paper due in 41 hours, Ana made her move over to Shari and her new friends to ask about the timeframe for departure. Shari essentially ignored her, giving one of those "just a few minutes" kind of looks. Knowing this meant nothing of significance, Ana stepped into the chilly air to consider a taxi or a long walk back to campus.

Going outside at that precise time in this precise area of the upper west side of Manhattan would prove to change her life forever.

This being well before the cell phone era, Ana found a lonely pay phone at the end of an eerily quiet New York City block. Digging for change with her gloves on, one of those life-altering moments presented itself. There was an innocuous-looking man of about Ana's age, walking with a woman who appeared much older than he, towards a taxi. Ana noticed them, but was far too shy to ask, as many New Yorkers do, to "split a cab."

Just then the man and woman noticed her and motioned for her to join them. Ana pretended to ignore them, but they kept waving their arms toward the cab. She looked around, glanced back into the bar window to notice Shari flirting more vivaciously than ever, and meandered out slowly toward the cab. Ana was nervous, but at the same time, figured that these two, plus the cab driver, looked safe enough.

Aside from the fact that the woman, who must have been closer to 40 than 30, was loud, incoherent and obnoxious, the ride was uneventful. Ana introduced herself, and the man told her he was Isaac. The woman's name was slurred so badly that it sounded like "Shoe-zet," and later Ana determined it to actually be Suzette.

Ana wanted to make small talk with the man, who seemed genuine and amicable enough, but he had his hands full, as though taking care of an infant, which is precisely how most inebriated folks appeared in Ana's mind. Being religious, Ana felt Isaac was a nice, old-fashioned name for a modern guy. Additionally, he was donning a shiny shirt, pressed pants and expensive looking black loafers. So she inquired.

Just as Isaac seemed ready to elaborate, Suzette began singing some incomprehensible Beatles song and the cab pulled to a stop. It was then Ana realized she had never told the cab driver where she was going and they were now much closer to mid-town than her area, a few miles back north. Isaac apologized and laughed, realizing what had occurred. "Give me a minute here, ok?" Isaac muttered uncomfortably as he helped stumbling Suzette out of the cab, up some stairs, and into an apartment building.

Ana figured it was his girlfriend, though she was unsure if they lived together, since Isaac had indicated his eventual return to the cab and their yet-to-begin conversation.

About three minutes later, Isaac came trotting back down the steps and into the vehicle.

"So, where were we? Anywhere yet?" Isaac asked, much more at ease now.

"Nowhere actually," Ana quipped back in her friendly way.

"Oh, well, oh yes, my name. It's biblical, I reckon. I mean, my parents and I, we're not overly religious, but they liked the name. Seemed historic and dignified."

Ana, realizing quickly that Isaac was witty, but at the same time mature, knew a great deal about the Old Testament and was interested in pressing further, but realized such was not a good time.

The cab driver looked back at them and cleared his throat, politely requesting attention the way a New York City cabbie might do.

Ana and Isaac looked at him, then each other, then laughed. Thankfully, Isaac spoke up.

"She lives at…."

Ana noted her address. Isaac looked intrigued. Ana was not sure if it was the address, or what, but he did catch Isaac glancing at her overall "look." Ana was a radiant and beautiful girl. No one denied this. She took after her mother, many said.

"Oh, wow. I'm sorry we took you all the way back down here. I should have figured you lived uptown since we were originally up there in the first place. I'm so sorry," he stated quite genteelly.

Ana, always confident intellectually, but often awkward socially, now wondered if Isaac's "intrigue" was over her address, her looks, both or neither.

Twelve minutes later or so---and not bad for Manhattan on a weekend night---Ana was about to step out of the cab, pay the driver and chalk up the night to experience, when Isaac piped in.

"At least let me buy you a drink now or sometime for all the trouble I've caused."

Ana, perhaps suspicious, declined.

"You may pay for the cab though," she said with a smile.

He nodded and smiled again. Ana noticed that he had long eyelashes and a very nice smile.

"Thanks," Ana yelled and walked toward her apartment, tired and stressed out, realizing she had not done any studying in hours.

As she looked back, Ana had almost expected some sort of a "Hollywood scene" where Isaac would step out and beg her to go out with him or be more persistent, but instead, here in the real world, the cab began to slowly pull away.

Just then, Isaac yelled in a very coy way.

"She's not my girlfriend. Never was…" And the cab rolled away.

Shari, who evidently had departed the pub soon after Ana, was half-asleep on the couch, but still lucid enough to have overheard Isaac's closing tidbit.

"Who was that?" Shari asked curiously.

Embarrassed, Ana looked down on her way to the bedroom, avoiding eye contact and answered tersely, "Oh, no one. Just a guy I shared a cab with."

Shari popped up like a dog running for its treat. She was as invidious as anyone Ana had known.

"Wait, you met a guy…at a bar…and you shared a cab…?

Ana tried to ignore her, sensing another jejune discussion on relationships with someone who'd never had one. She instead focused her attention on the most recent phone bill. But Shari pressed on.

"This is not an everyday occurrence, Ana Mendez. What's his name?" Shari asked, getting more excited by the moment.

"Isaac. And he really *is* just a guy I shared a cab with," Ana answered, looking to end the conversation as soon as possible.

"Are you going to go out with him?" Shari pondered, desperately hoping for an affirmation from Ana.

"I doubt it," Ana replied. "We didn't exchange numbers."

"Well, he knows where you live," Shari muttered with a smirk, and was off to her room.

Shari was right.

Two mornings later, Ana was slipping on some ice as she left the apartment for class when a yellow note caught her eye.

Needless to say, it was from the mysterious Isaac, asking her out for "coffee or whatever sometime soon." Vague as he was, he did leave his number.

With the advice of Shari, Ana decided to wait a day, call, and politely decline. It seemed silly, as this would mean Ana risked pushing Isaac away quickly and decisively. But Shari, who had had her share of relationships, was adamant.

Ana called Isaac the next evening, followed Shari's advice, and was pleasantly surprised by how Isaac very confidently said, "Ok, next time then."

It wasn't as though Ana had given him a direct "never," but she had not left the door open for a "next time."

Three days later, on Saturday morning at 9:30am, Isaac called. Asleep, Ana cleared her throat to speak and was delighted to hear that Isaac, unlike most collegians and grad students she knew, was not only awake, but peppy. Ana was not necessarily a morning person, but still arose earlier than most she knew and admired those who could pull themselves up at a reasonable hour, especially on the weekend.

Whether serious or not, Isaac invited her to an "early lunch" somewhere near Central Park that day. Quick on her game, Ana told him she was a tad busy, but that meeting up at a local café she knew "near campus" that crisp afternoon would be better for her. Isaac accepted.

Twenty-seven months later they were engaged.

Forty-five months later, on Thanksgiving Weekend 1989, Isaac and Ana Hyde became husband and wife.

2

Dreary November days on the island of Manhattan can drag on forever. The sun, after rising ever so briefly, if at all, disappears as quickly as the daylight, and by 4pm, dusk is setting in. A day that begins in darkness easily ends the same, as most New York City workers seldom return home before six in the evening.

Isaac Hyde was no exception. As the Public and Military Historian for the Museum of Twentieth Century History on Manhattan's upper west side---not far from where he and Ana had their first official date more than 20 years ago---Isaac served as Director of Research, thus regularly worked ten hour days, without the pay to match such hearty effort.

Isaac had worked at this museum since 1984, a month after he graduated from Clarkson. There was no baseball career, no grad school, and surely no "year to find himself" in Europe like many of his wealthy classmates. With his father's help, Isaac had to repay school loans, and eventually assist both his parents when they retired and moved to Arizona a decade or so later.

He loved the job at first, was promoted twice before he was 30, but had now occupied the same position for nearly 15 years. The workload though, by virtue of being at a history museum, was somewhat monotonous. Isaac was an expert on America's history from the end of the Spanish American War until the onset of the Korean War. He also gave tours, presentations, spoke with the media and numerous dignitaries, and had often been recognized with accolades from magazines and historical societies. He had traveled quite a bit, mostly domestic, but his pay did not seem to rise fast enough to meet his current life costs, especially with college tuition for two children now visible on the life's horizon.

The Executive Director of the museum, by virtue of having his PhD, made the "big" money" and had the ego to match. It apparently didn't matter to anyone that his Doctorate was in something called "Post Colonial Studies," a modern creation of the university system that had more to do with castigating America's proud history and focusing on the "social impact" of war, than the nuts and bolts, like military strategy or the Great Depression.

With his Doctorate, Greg, who at 37, was younger than Isaac, seemed content with his role (and salary) as Director, as did the powers-that-be in New York City's "Museum Hierarchy," as Isaac and other co-workers called it. And nothing was going to change this it seemed. Isaac surely wasn't indolent in his time there, but it was clear, wrongly or rightly, that he was not moving upward in the system anytime soon. Isaac Hyde was approaching middle age, and was in no mood for a "mid life crisis," but was also honest enough to acknowledge this was a plateau he had to move beyond. Ana, with her Masters, surely agreed.

But this took Isaac some time to rationalize. Here he was, at a high position at a nationally-known museum in America's biggest city, with knowledge of 20th century American history that made his colleagues envious; but, due solely to reasons of financial security, he was considering actually spending money and time getting an additional diploma he felt he did not need. The Hydes, with their two incomes, weren't impecunious either; therefore, Isaac was miffed by this impasse.

"Quite a world we live in here in 2007," he whined to Ana one night.

"Well, the value of a college degree is watered down these days," Ana confessed. "But this could also be a chance for you to learn and broaden your horizons."

"Broaden horizons." "Watered down." Boy, those words sure sounded "clinical" coming from his wife who worked in a clinic all day.

Moreover, Isaac really had no idea what that meant. Of course he knew the cliché, but fumbled over what Ana was intimating, if anything, over the next few days, as November rolled into December and the holidays approached.

The holidays for the Hyde family, like any folks living away from the rest of their families, was often complicated. Isaac was very schedule oriented and enjoyed the logistics of holiday planning; but each year, especially as their parents simultaneously grew older, it became a tad more tedious to make everyone happy.

In the past decade since Isaac's folks relocated to Arizona, it was nearly impossible to see them and Ana's parents in Indiana during the same time frame, though they once completed that feat a few years back. When David and Sarah Hyde were still just a four-hour spin down I-95 prior to 1997, it was easy to pay a visit, then hop on a plane a few days later (or occasionally make the ten hour drive) to Indiana for a celebration with Ana's gregarious relatives.

That Isaac was Jewish and Ana Catholic was never a huge deal. They focused on celebrating the season and spending time with loved ones.

If there was a Hanukkah menorah in the Hyde home or a Christmas tree in the Mendez home, no one took offense. If Ana's parents spoke Spanish to their relatives, Isaac would try to listen and join in the conversation. Over the years, his Spanish became nearly fluent. If Isaac's folks wanted to "do Jewish things," as Ana said when they ate traditional meals or said Hebrew blessings, Ana was polite enough to attempt to join in as well.

The two families even celebrated the holidays all together one year, which, overall, went as well as could be expected. Both Isaac's Jewish family and Ana's Hispanic Catholic family were full of life, convivial chatter and even introspection. All respected one another, tried to understand the cultural and religious differences, and refrain from any unwelcome stereotypes. It was a nice mix. But of course, as Hanukkah's eight days and Christmas seldom overlapped, this occurrence would be rare.

In their private lives though, religion had been a difficult dilemma for Isaac and Ana as they considered marriage and then children. But it was one that, with the help of calm discourse, honesty, tolerance, advice from others, reading books, doing workbooks, and simple experience, they had managed to "survive."

While both came from pious families, Ana was more devout, and was also the mother. This meant that Jewish tradition dictated the children would always be Catholic, unless she converted. Thus, Isaac compromised, and the children were predominantly raised in the Catholic faith; though, since Ana was knowledgeable and enthusiastic about Judaism from her Catholic upbringing, the children always knew that not only was their father Jewish, but what that meant and why. Both Isaac and Ana felt the children seemed better off this way, rather than being "cultural Jews" who therefore miss the meaning of why they are Jewish completely.

Ana once mused that she could not fathom how so many Jews were totally secular, thus missing out on the glorious history of the "Chosen People" and how this moniker came to be. She, like other Catholics she knew, was always taught to lend a debt of gratitude towards Jews for providing the roots of their own Christian faith. Once at high holiday temple services, when Ana saw numerous Jews chatting and ignoring Yom Kippur's holiest prayers, she asked Isaac not only why these people bothered to attend if it's more of a social event, but what makes them Jewish if they don't adhere to, or admire, the customs and traditions? This was a topic long discussed, and not necessarily explained by "watered down" Judaism's popular denominations like the Reform Movement, but one Isaac indeed enjoyed exploring, studying at work and writing about in his spare time.

One decision that was never an option for the Hyde family was dual religion. The kids would need one religion to dominate and the other to survive, be respected and understood. Neither parent sought secularism or atheism, which is what often occurs when both religions are given to the child by parents who seemingly do not comprehend that this simply does not work.

And so the holidays, as one would expect, brought questions from both Ana's and Isaac's parents about his prospects, as the Hyde's spent the Christmas holiday in the Indianapolis area. Isaac's parents then gave their grandchildren the pleasure of a semi-unannounced visit to the Hyde home in New Jersey and a few more days of family functions in New York City.

Ana's parents did not know of Isaac's so-called dilemma, but much to his chagrin, Ana mentioned Isaac's "predicament" to her parents, seeking advice. The Mendezes didn't want to pry nor interfere so they said they supported either decision. All of a sudden Isaac realized that, whether he liked it or not, there was a decision that now in fact needed to be made.

How quickly things were moving.

January beckoned, and Isaac recalled that most deadlines for the few graduate programs he had looked into were at the end of February or earlier. He was suddenly seeing shades of his 1980 college application process with his parents pestering him constantly. This was quite unwelcome.

Days after these annoying memories passed through Isaac's mind while sitting in the small but warm Mendez house on Christmas Night enjoying good food and football on television, David and Sarah Hyde, now fully aware of their son's next step in life---in his 45th year---were sitting on Isaac's living room couch peppering Isaac with questions and advice as only two Jewish parents could.

"You're a smart kid," said David. "You should get your Masters at a top notch school like an Ivy or at least Brandeis or NYU. At NYU you could live at home."

"Isaac, if people are pushing you into things you don't want, what about a different field?" his mother asked as she put on an additional sweater. "You could go into law, teaching or business. Could Ana turn up the heat in here?"

"We have no connections in those fields," David interrupted abruptly. "He's a writer, like I was." This he said proudly with an affirming nod toward his son, who turned to his mom for the next word, knowing this would not be a brief discussion.

"Well, your cousin----oh never mind," Sarah stopped, looking frustrated. "Isaac honey, are you doing this because you want to, or because you have to?"

Isaac knew that unless he wanted to change careers or risk being fired, he *had* to get his Masters. He also knew that his mom had to hear that he *wanted* to do this, even if he really did not.

"Both," he replied.

Sarah seemed relieved.

"Well, then you need to go to a good program," David quipped.

"I agree. And close by," Sarah said.

Isaac told his parents that, of course close by would be good, but the name of the school is not as important as for other graduate degrees; rather the reputability of the program was paramount. His Masters would be in Military History, a program being phased out of many schools due to the more "progressive" education that had infested itself in the past few decades in American education. Isaac had his own views on this and had done a great deal of writing bemoaning the fact, but saved those opinions for other times.

Secondly, due to the scarcity of the programs, he might have no choice but to enroll somewhere not near the Tri State Area. This would be the hardest part, and he and Ana had not broached the subject often, nor shared much with their children, Lauren, who was in 8th grade, and Ross, who was in 4th.

Isaac also had to take the Graduate Records Examination shortly after the holidays, which would determine much about his options and ultimate fate. That was the next step, and Isaac informed his parents of all the aforementioned as well. As David and Sarah flew back to Arizona just after to New Years, they seemed to understand as best they could. Isaac added, in a half-joking way as they boarded the plane,

"Hey, maybe I'll go to school in the Phoenix area and live with you guys." They all shared a nice laugh.

Isaac, however, had the pressure now to make some life-altering decisions.

3

Isaac scored rather well on his GRE. He never told anyone---not even Ana---his actual scores, but they were very high, especially in the writing portion. Part of Isaac wanted to boast, but another part acknowledged he was 45 years old, worked in an academic, white-collar profession, and was taking an exam in a field he loved, where most around him were college seniors; therefore shouldn't he have done exceedingly well?

Isaac was not an intellectual elitist, thus, though he rarely discussed it with Ana, had never been in awe of her Bachelors degree from Notre Dame nor her Masters from Columbia, even when some of her friends gushed. Nonetheless, with his top tier GRE scores and eagerness to add another notch to his resume, Isaac began pouring over books and the internet, seeing at what highly-regarded school he could apply for his Masters in Military History.

Considering what he had read about for years, Isaac was not surprised he did not see one Ivy League school nor any upper crust liberal arts colleges offering said program. In fact, precious few schools did at all. Isaac had read articles in respected magazines like *The National Review* and *Commentary* lamenting the loss of military history from the undergrad curriculum, much less as a major or graduate field of study.

Theories abound, but the most accepted one was that, the arrival of the baby boomer generation as Department Chairmen in the 80s and 90s precipitated this change. With their antipathy toward war and the military lingering, these professors had let the older military history professors retire, *without renewing their Chair.* The money and positions then went where these Vietnam era relics desired: "social history" and counter-culture fields like "American Studies," "Post Colonial Studies," and other majors non-existent before the 1980s. Isaac's view was that this was un-American and a shame, but he couldn't concern himself with that right now; he needed a grad school to attend.

Weeks of research done, the month of January nearing its end, and most schools' deadlines four weeks away at most, Isaac had narrowed his "field" down to five schools:

Ohio University

Syracuse University

West Virginia University

The University of Delaware

The University of Minnesota

In creating this compendium, Isaac had ruled out just about all private schools due to exorbitant costs, especially since his employer would only assist with 50% of tuition and none of the travel, room or board.

As Isaac looked over the positives and negatives of the five universities with Ana and Lauren night after night, he finally narrowed his choices down to two: Delaware and Ohio.

Syracuse had been eventually ruled out solely based upon cost. It had been included because it was only a four hour drive from home, but was not plausible when all was said, considered and done.

Minnesota, though perhaps the most known and respected program of the lot, was too far and too cold. It was in the heart of Minneapolis/ Saint Paul, and Isaac longed for a school in a classic "college town." Though Clarkson was in a small, quaint town, there was another school in Potsdam, and the athletics and size of city did not equal a "rah rah" college town. Ana and Lauren scoffed at a 45 year old man caring about such things, but knowing Isaac for 24 and 14 years respectively, they understood.

Morgantown, West Virginia, was a fun and lovely college town which the Hydes had visited and passed through on various road trips, but the reputation was not great, especially in the northeast. WVU was therefore eliminated, somewhat to Isaac's chagrin, as well as Ross's, who was a big fan of their athletic teams, mostly to spite Isaac who had become a University of Pittsburgh fan sometime in the past decade or so.

Thus, Delaware and Ohio. To Isaac the Historian, it sounded like a tale of George Washington and the French-Indian War, but this was real, current life.

Both universities were in college towns, yet Athens, Ohio, was "only" a scenic, mountainous seven or eight hour ride from the Hyde residence in New Jersey. This would make plane travel unnecessary and give Isaac, a lover of driving, a chance to come home on a whim.

Newark, home of the University of Delaware, was an even easier drive. Isaac and nearly everyone he knew had passed through the charming town off I-95 on their way from Washington DC to Philadelphia or New York or vice versa. It was very well located, just a poke over two hours from the house, 90 minutes from Washington DC and an hour from Philly.

But Newark seemed dull as compared to Athens. It wasn't hilly enough, nor rustic nor exotic, though Isaac chuckled at thinking of a town in southeastern Ohio as "exotic." It was just that Newark was as urban as you could get in a pleasant town, since it was so close to three major American cities. Almost too close. You could get New York, Philly and D.C. television and radio stations there after all.

Athens was remote. In addition to being close enough but surely far enough from New York, it was:

Three short hours from Pittsburgh, one of Isaac's favorite cities.

Three hours from Cleveland.

Four hours from Indianapolis, which he reiterated to Ana, in the hopes she'd believe him when he said he'd visit her parents at least twice during the school year.

Five and a half hours from the Nation's Capital.

90 minutes from Columbus, Ohio, the nearest major city.

And just two windy hours from Morgantown, where Isaac promised Ross he'd meet him for a basketball or football game during the year… if Ana would drive him the 375 miles each way. It was a beautiful ride, Isaac promised. But Ana was not Isaac in that department.

Either way, the decision came down to money, family and the future. After another week comparing and evaluating the schools, the votes were tabulated from all the "precincts."

Ana voted for Delaware. Lauren for Ohio, as did Ross, though their vote counted for just one. Ana's younger brother and her parents went for Ohio, counting that as one total as well. David chose Delaware, and Sarah chose Ohio. That made it three to two for Ohio, but Isaac promised he'd consider his best friend since college, Jason, as a vote. Jason, who had grown up in Aberdeen, Maryland, "just a stone's throw across the Susquehanna" from Delaware, as he often claimed, chose UD for that reason -- so he wasn't necessarily a fair vote. But it did make it three to three. Isaac thought of this as the seventh game of the real life World Series and he would decide the winner.

Thoughts ruminated through his mind for a few nights, but then he decided; he would be a Bobcat. Even though it was only a year, the town and location were more his style. Isaac planned to mail his acceptance letter to the Ohio University tomorrow from work.

But, as the cliché goes, a funny thing happened on the way (to the post office).

Actually, it occurred in two parts: once on the way to the post office and once that evening.

Isaac had his letter of intent ready to be mailed with priority to Athens, Ohio, from the mid-town Manhattan post office near his museum, but when he went to send it out during his lunch hour, the place was jammed with lines deep into the halls. Frustrated, hungry, and with, by his math, two more days to spare before his application would be late and subject to a fine and perhaps worse, Isaac decided to return to mail it tomorrow since his local post office would be closed by the time he arrived home.

The second "funny thing" was the mysterious letter with the postmark of Knoxville, Tennessee, that greeted Isaac on his kitchen counter that evening.

Isaac, thinking it was junk mail, was ready to toss it into the circular file, when he noticed that under the bright orange Tennessee logo was indicia that the letter came from the "Volunteer Department of Military History."

Volunteer? Isaac was perplexed. He didn't want to volunteer at a campus history center or museum, especially in the state of Tennessee. But the letter also noted "Department of Military History," so he tore the envelope open.

The semi-glossy and very official letter read as follows:

Dear Mr. Hyde:

As part of an ongoing collaborative effort between the dwindling number of universities offering a Masters degree in the study of Military History, the University of Tennessee at Knoxville was made aware of your applications to other programs. We are thus legally permitted to send you the following letter of interest.

The University of Tennessee-Knoxville is nationally known as a leader in the education of our nation's role during wartime. The graduate program in military history, an extensive one year consisting of a full class load, has a reputation for its breadth and a dignified, experienced faculty. Without going into further detail, at this point, we are very interested in reviewing your application for admission. By signing this document, you are giving us permission to do such. We will then be in touch with you if your qualifications meet our standards.

You are under no obligation to grant us permission, nor does your acceptance of this letter's request indicate you wish to enroll. However, we look forward to hearing from you and anticipate you would be an important asset to the University of Tennessee. If you desire to be a part of the great Volunteer tradition, please don't hesitate to contact us.

A few portions of this letter jumped out at Isaac, causing him not to immediately discard it.

Firstly, even if they were exaggerating, a "nationally known leader" in military history on his resume couldn't hurt matters. Also, the simple wording of the letter---and the fact that he was being sought out---comforted Isaac. He quickly jumped on the internet to look more into the University of Tennessee's main campus.

Two hours later, Isaac had poured through as much of the school and program's site as he possibly could tolerate, and he was exhausted. He was also rather pleased. Only two items still befuddled and irked him.

One was what to tell Ana and their debate that would follow, especially after the weeks and weeks of discussing his initial application process and the final decision that ultimately followed just days ago. Don't forget that Ana was under the impression Isaac had mailed his acceptance to Ohio that afternoon.

The second was the state of Tennessee itself. Isaac had actually driven across the length of Tennessee on Interstate 40 many years back, and had since visited Nashville, Chattanooga and Memphis, and had enjoyed the former two quite well. His memories of Knoxville though, were quite opaque. He had been twice, once as a child with his parents after touring the Great Smoky Mountains National Park, and the other time by himself on a cross country drive, but that was nearly 20 years ago.

Should he visit prior? There was no time, as the letter indicated that time was in fact of the essence. Isaac also needed to fill out the entire application and submit such by March 14, as the university had already given him this deadline. One good aspect, however, was that Isaac had gleaned his acceptance was a near certainty.

Ana arrived home that night in a bad mood. Isaac had seen this situation present itself sporadically for nearly two decades now, but also knew that he had to mention the "situation" at some point.

A few hours, a family dinner prepared by Isaac, and two glasses of wine later, Isaac and Ana lay on the couch with the kids asleep. This seemed to be the right moment.

Ana was closing a rant about how stressful dealing with certain clients can be and how she longed to have Isaac's "opportunity" to "get away" for a bit, when she said, "Well, you are lucky. And though I am in a bad mood, I am unselfish and therefore happy for you. At least the acceptance is in the mail and we have some closure."

The Hydes both thrived on "closure," so while Ana suddenly looked relaxed and Isaac did not, she gave him a discerning look.

Before she could ask, Isaac said quickly, "There was a very long line today, so I did not mail it…"

Ana smiled and said, "Well, you have two more days. Just do it tomorrow."

But Isaac had to tell her the truth at this point; he did not plan to mail the application. Not only that, he had to tell her about Tennessee.

"What, why not?" she pleaded. "I wanted us to be done with all this, finally."

"Well, we're not," Isaac said delicately but optimistically. "I think we have another option, and perhaps a better one."

For the next hour, Isaac went into salesman mode, attempting to convince Ana of the program in Knoxville's merit, all the while further convincing himself that this was the school for him.

The Hydes went to bed that night, exhausted but a bit more settled.

But in the morning, knowing this was "D-Day" in his historical mind, Isaac wanted to officially confirm that this was the right choice. Ana seemed exhausted by the whole ordeal, so her "yes" seemed more out of fatigue than confidence. Isaac knew as well as she did that this decision could have a substantial impact upon the family's well-being, not just for the coming year but deep into the future, so he needed to be sure in his mind.

Realizing a phone call to David and Sarah out in Arizona would just prolong the agony, Isaac decided against that idea. Knowing his children were on their way to school and likely would not quite understand the gravity of the situation, he did not seek their approval. But not wanting to make a capricious decision, though the timing required such, Isaac went to his Rabbi for advice. Afterwards, he sought out the priest where he, Ana and the children attended Church in his ecumenical family.

Both gave somewhat generic yet positive advice about pursuing the path that would make him and his family most content. If he and Ana didn't have children, the decision would be easy, but such was not the case. The "most content" thing to do was to stay put, but that was no longer an option. Nonetheless, the advice assuaged Isaac's concerns, for no one had told him what he feared: that he was making a grave mistake---either by heading to the "Deep South," or by "deserting" his family for life in another region of the country for the next nine months.

Isaac deposited his note of interest to the UTK Masters program in the mail the next morning as he arrived to work, essentially sealing his fate. He knew what they had to offer and was intent upon accepting admission, which would surely be the next item to come. Isaac's research had provided him with a glowing view of the school, program, campus life, people, and most importantly, Tennessee's more than nominal financial aid, which helped foment his eagerness to enroll, and become a "Volunteer," so to speak.

4

Lauren Hyde was a good girl. An eighth grader with the maturity of a high school senior but also the opinionated personality to boot, she was a joy to raise, while at the same time a handful. Not necessarily materialistic like many of her ilk, she was studious and independent, but could ruffle some feathers if need be, especially being student council president in her last year of middle school. Her ego, soon to likely be squashed on day one of high school, was currently, as Ana liked to say "effusive," or basically unrestrained. It saw no limits. She was, as Isaac once bemoaned, the typical middle-class eighth grade girl, for better or worse.

Ross Hyde was, for *better*, the typical 4th grade boy. Like his dad, he loved sports, and as he steamrolled toward middle school, had begun to enjoy history and writing just like his dad and grandpa. He was a joy to be around a majority of the time.

But what effect would Isaac's move have on the children?

Isaac was more concerned about Lauren's entry into high school, not just socially but academically. Being in an "academic" field, he knew public education was not what it once was. Without getting into the actual curriculum, Isaac knew would be thrust upon her without recourse by "educators," he wanted to be as involved as possible. Isaac, like Ana, believed it was important for parents to diligently keep track of their student's classes, find out what was being taught or not taught by the teachers, and clarify material given to their children. In 2009, more than ever, they felt it was important to protect the "investment" they've entrusted to the State as their child moved toward college and lack of parental control.

Being the psychologist and constant analyst, Ana theorized in sundry ways. When Isaac pressed her for the short version, she said the obvious answer would be that Lauren's maturity and resilience would shield her from any disappointment, and if she had any, she'd hide it fairly well. Ross, however, would be despondent to lose his "buddy," even if just for a few months at a time and less than a year overall.

Despite discussions, Isaac and Ana both admitted they had no idea how their offspring would react. The Hydes hoped for something of a happy medium at best, with only one child having difficulties adjusting, especially with Ana being the only adult in the house for the coming school year. Any truculent behavior from either child would make her job at home and at work much more difficult, even for a strong, mature woman such as she.

The wait and see game would have to be just that.

During the summer months, Isaac made every effort to accommodate his children's needs. He was, as he put it, "super dad." Though admittedly some of it was out of guilt brought on by his impending absence, he reveled in having his children's adoration, especially Ross, whom he took to numerous sporting events and enjoyed some "male bonding." And though Lauren was a post-pubescent teen without a drivers' license or much in common with her father---and a social calendar comparable to any adult's to boot--- she and Isaac were able to enjoy each other's company most of the time.

In late August, on one of the last days prior to Isaac's departure for Knoxville, the Hyde family went for the classic American activity, especially in the northeast: a trip to the beach.

As Isaac read up on some "stimulating" history (an assessment of the final demise of the Spanish Empire during the late 19th century), Ross played paddle ball with some boy he ran into from school. Ana read her book alongside Lauren, who was reading from *Seventeen*. The Hyde family looked and felt at peace. Then, as Isaac feared it would at some point prior to his ultimate departure, it happened:

"Dad, seriously, do you really have to go?" Ross asked innocently.

Admittedly hoping to avoid a detailed discussion, Isaac calmly said, "Well, it just has to be that way for a short time." He knew that Ross and Lauren both understood the reasons for his entering the Masters program and what it would eventually mean, positively, for the family. But they were disappointed, as most children would be.

"Yep, it just has to be," stated Ana, somewhat sarcastically, catching Isaac off guard. Isaac sensed Ana had suddenly decided to let her true feelings out, which was okay, but in front of the kids?

Then Lauren chimed in, as only she knew how.

"Well, it's selfish and unfair, if you ask me," she claimed.

This was priceless coming from Lauren, Isaac mused silently. Here was your typical 14 year-old girl who basically acted as though her father hardly existed, unless he was driving her to meet up with her friends; but she knew how to push buttons, so she partook.

Ross looked on, seemingly in thought.

"Do we need to talk about this now, or at all?" Isaac asked Lauren. "I mean, we've been through this multiple times for the past ten months, with a decision having been made nearly five months ago.... and where on earth did you get that bathing suit. Cover up." Lauren mostly ignored his words, and walked toward the ocean in an outfit too revealing for dad.

They all knew Isaac was right---on both accounts, actually---but he also knew it was easy for him to treat the situation cavalierly.

Isaac probably should have ended the argument right there, or had a non-combative response, but he foolishly did not. He regretted what he said next.

"Well, for once, this is about daddy," he noted strongly. "Daddy needs to take care of himself and the family will benefit in the end."

Ana looked especially dumbfounded by what he said. Lauren turned around and walked back toward the group.

"Kids, he did not mean that," she said.

"I meant it, though not in a selfish way," Isaac explained feebly. "This is the right thing to do."

A peccadillo of Isaac's was his quick reactions to matters and his insatiable desire to "resolve" an issue once he personally deemed it over.

Just as the three other Hydes turned to verbally berate the patriarch of the clan, something occurred that normally would have caused Isaac great ire as a father, but this time he welcomed it.

One of Lauren's female friends came running up and asked her if she wanted to hang out at some "party" that night. Lauren excitedly agreed, then condescendingly looked over at her dad for permission. Isaac nodded.

She grabbed her friend's hand and screamed with joy, "Dad, you're the best!" The bipolar personality of a teenager had come to the rescue.

"A co-ed party?" Ana asked. The Hydes were fairly conservative in most walks of life, but no more conservative on these types of issues than any parents of a girl about to enter high school.

"Mom, I'm a week from being in high school," Lauren said. "Of course, but it'll be cool. Chelsea's parents will there."

Chelsea, who looked older than Lauren, and who Isaac didn't recognize, explained to the Hydes this was the case. And then Isaac, seeing the angle to get out of the tense debate that had just begun, said "Ok, yep, sounds fine. Be home by midnight though, 'Ren."

Ana gave Isaac a knowing look, but that was that.

"I ended the *tsuris*," Isaac bragged. "That's Yiddish for 'aggravation,' especially the minor type."

Ana gave Isaac a frown, but then moved on in thought.

Ross was back in the ocean with his friend, and Lauren seemed on cloud nine via the end of summer party she was invited to join. She skipped away again, this time with Chelsea.

The funny thing was that the last argument Isaac, Ana and Lauren had was at the end of the school year when a boy-girl party presented itself, and Lauren was finally granted permission to attend after quite the show of begging. Here she had won easily for obvious reasons. Either way, Lauren Hyde was clever.

"We'll talk later," Ana said sternly to Isaac. He gave her a look, but nodded, and quickly buried his head in his book.

Ironically, that was one topic Isaac was relieved to be avoiding when he departed: Lauren's 9th grade year. He had heard the horror stories about boy-girl parties and older boys with younger girls in high school. And, well, Lauren took after her mother in the "good looks" department. A daughter of a mixed-race couple, both of considerable attractiveness, she was very pretty and quite physically developed for her age. She had a boyfriend most of eighth grade, who was the son of a family friend, and thus, very trustworthy as far as the Hydes knew. But high school and its parties were a whole other animal. Isaac worried, but trusted Ana to stand guard against anything unwanted. After all, Ana had been raised far more strictly than Isaac. He just wished since he could not be there, that Lauren had an older brother protecting her. But alas, she certainly did not.

As for Ross, the opposite was the case. Isaac was hardly concerned with his energetic, happy, popular, intelligent, athletic ten-year-old boy as he began fifth grade that fall. Despite warnings, he was far from concerned about Ross having any "emotional traumas" while his dad was away for months at a time. If he did, Isaac was sure Ana could handle it just as well as he could. In a few years it might be tougher, but this year seemed the "perfect year" in Ross's life, if there ever was one, for dad to be away for awhile. While Lauren might have issues, those would be female problems, which Ana would be adept as possible at quelling, and Isaac would probably exacerbate such maladies anyway. On the other hand, Ross would be fine, and in the end, everyone would be brought closer together by Isaac's absence, perhaps. As the cliché goes, absence makes the heart grow fonder.

Ready or not, on to Knoxville it was.

5

"D-day," so to speak, was the last Saturday in August. It was a week prior to Labor Day, so Isaac would be missing the holiday weekend, which was unfortunately one of the Hyde family's favorite holidays. But classes began the ensuing Monday, so a one-day drive down and a weekend to prepare himself and his new living arrangements (a one bedroom apartment in the hills above the campus Isaac had selected over the internet) seemed appropriate.

It was a humid, glistening Saturday morning in the New Jersey suburbs, meaning, in Isaac's weather mind, that it would be brutal down in Knoxville, 700 miles to the southwest. Nonetheless, it was clear and he had a drive ahead of him. And frankly, after the teary good-byes, Isaac was looking forward to it.

As a younger man, Isaac would often "lose himself" in drives across America's historic and pleasant roads, on his own, in his beat up car, staying in crummy motels and eating cheap food. And not that marriage had deprived him of such occurrences, but when he now took road trips, he was rarely alone. Isaac also seldom traveled for work, and if he did, these were short trips, often no further than a couple hundred miles on a single day. Moreover, with two kids and a wife, accommodations had to be upgraded, as did his car.

On this trip though, and for the next year, Ana would keep Isaac's modern Nissan Altima in New Jersey, while Isaac would have to make do with Ana's small, sporty and very effeminate, Mazda something. Isaac never did quite know what model it was, but since it was red, especially with "northern" plates, he'd have to watch his speed and driving style as he motored down Interstate 81 well south of the Mason-Dixon Line.

Some emotional, but not unnecessary lengthy good-byes occurred in the Hyde's small driveway and then Isaac was off. The cliché yet sad site of his family farther away was in his rear view as he hopped onto Highway 78 and cruised west toward the Delaware River and Pennsylvania state line.

Though Isaac wanted to enjoy his ride, he felt weird about leaving for such a long time. This stretch would also be his longest away from the family, as the 700 mile ride would mean he'd likely not return home before Thanksgiving. He was still holding out hope that Ana would take him up on the idea to meet for some fall color viewing in Virginia, or a meeting in Washington DC, but that was yet to be confirmed.

Was Isaac a bad person? Would he not recognize his children when he next saw their faces? The answer to both rhetorical questions was likely "no." As for the latter, surely Ross wouldn't "age" much in the first quarter of fifth grade, but Lauren was growing too fast physically and emotionally for his liking, and he worried about the lack of an adult male figure in her life when boys came to call. But then again, Ana had female experience in these matters, and could be as tough as anyone with dicey or unwelcome social situations.

As for whether he was wrong to choose this direction, Isaac had talked with everyone over and over; he and Ana had countless arguments, seen social workers, had meaningful discourse, and read material from those who had dealt with similar predicaments. Their conclusions were pliant when necessary, but steadfast when it mattered most. The Hydes had also consulted the family's priest as well as their local rabbi. The two had prayed on the situation before sleeping certain nights. And here Isaac was, traveling west with the morning sun still rising behind him, asking G-d if he was a "bad man." Introspection seemed necessary. Isaac Hyde had learned how deleterious decisions could become when made in a whimsical fashion. He was not one of those people. And that, he often mused, was for the better.

But as Isaac headed off into this morning soaked warm with summer in central New Jersey---one of the prettier parts of a fairly bland state---he knew his family also wouldn't want him to dwell, even if they were. Isaac had been told over and over by his family, his parents and friends that he should make the best of this situation. Many middle-aged men, including some of Isaac's buddies, would kill to be away for such an extended period of time in a more-relaxed environment. His current and future employers could care less what kind of grades he'd make, so long as the end result was a degree. And Isaac Hyde loved the open road. And here it was, presenting itself in all its glory, right in front of him, for the entire day. Fields on all sides displayed sprouting corn and soybeans. G-d bless America indeed, he mused. And with that, Isaac gunned the Mazda Protégé (yes, Protégé; he finally recalled that was the model of Ana's car) up to 70 and propelled himself toward the Delaware River.

6

Pennsylvania is a rustic, hilly, and scenic state when you're not in Philadelphia, and Isaac began to remember this as he moved west on Interstate 78 toward the central part of the state and its capital in Harrisburg. Sadly, Isaac had no time to explore the impeccable Amish Country, historic Valley Forge, the Gettysburg region and other beauties in the Keystone State, as he finally headed due south once he crossed the mighty Susquehanna River and picked up 81 in Harrisburg.

To history and travel "nerds" like Isaac, there is a unique part of I-81 about an hour southwest of Harrisburg where you traverse four US states in no more than 40 miles. Isaac recalled it from passing through going north years back while returning on a road trip with Ana from the Smokey Mountains. And now, as he crossed the Pennsylvania state line into Maryland, he began his trek into and through "The South." Well, to a northerner, he was in the south. To do this though, Isaac passed over the historic "Mason Dixon Line": a dividing line mostly between the Keystone and Old Line State. In fact, the "Line" actually forms part of the borders of not just Pennsylvania and Maryland, but Delaware and West Virginia, which was part of Virginia until 1863. It was surveyed between 1763 and 1767 by Charles Mason and Jeremiah Dixon in the resolution of a border dispute between British colonies in Colonial America. The Line later served to define slave and free states, and now is used in more of a cultural sense to divide north from south in the US. But that was just what was ruminating through Isaac's brain.

As this was a thin edge of Maryland's western portions, within miles, the Mazda was in a sliver of West Virginia, and then, lastly, Virginia, as the south truly now beckoned, even though Isaac was technically still north of Washington DC. The heat was suddenly stifling, and Isaac rolled up the windows to turn on the air conditioning as he entered the Confederacy.

This southwesterly portion of Interstate 81 is a great American road that moves along through the heart of the Appalachian Mountain range. Virginia's Blue Ridge portion is to the west, with the verdant pasture of the historic Shenandoah Valley to the east and the Nation's Capital lying just 60 miles due east, but far, far away culturally. Virginia leaves its hills pristine, with homes down in the valley below, as opposed to other Appalachian states like Pennsylvania and West Virginia, where many houses dot the hills.

As Isaac saw names of Civil War towns like Winchester, Staunton, Chancellorsville and eventually farther down, Fredericksburg, he began to ponder the legacy of the Confederacy, specifically the celebrated General Robert E. Lee. Lee and others under his command had won key battles in all of these sites, mostly during the winter of 1862 and the following summer as the Confederacy pushed north toward Harrisburg before Lee was repelled in the pivotal battle of Gettysburg by the Union. Nearly 50,000 men died on July 1, 2 and 3 of 1863, in the only true full-scale battle on union soil during the War Between the States.

At his museum in New York City, Isaac, despite being raised in the North just like his colleagues, was deemed a "Southern Sympathizer" since Isaac knew his history well enough to be honest about the nobility of General like Robert E. Lee. Isaac was the de facto "head historian," seniority-wise, and without saying it aloud found the views of his co-workers on this specific topic to be ignorant and bereft of facts. They'd roll their eyes when Isaac would admit that in many ways the south was a "better-trained army" and that the north only triumphed because, in the end, they had more men and money. This was factual, and did not dismiss the immoral practice of slavery that northerners, *after 1863*, were fighting to eradicate. But Isaac felt it of utmost importance to tell all of history's stories, and not revisionist or irresponsible history.

Most of his colleagues were younger and educated at elite universities where a positive word about Confederates was far less common than gracious comments about Communists or Radical Islam. Like them, Isaac had been educated in the politically correct era of "higher education" but had read enough *outside* of class, from both sides, to rectify the tendentious views of his professors. Most others, naturally, had not. Recent polls showed that over 85 percent of professors voted one way in the most recent presidential election, and that was over 90 percent at the "best" universities of America (Ivy League, small private colleges). Fully half of university students, according to recent polling, admitted professors foist their socio-political views upon collegians for no reason. In turn, over one-third feared their grades would be lowered if they did not agree with their professors' one-sided views. Isaac was disgruntled that universities, supposedly a place of tolerance, questioning and debate, had become a place where so-called academics had plenary powers. Didn't they consider the suppression of opposing views, especially toward young people, reminiscent of Fascism? Isaac did, but he also proudly held different ideas than most 21st century historians.

As Isaac cruised off on his year away from Manhattan and said revisionism from his fellow historians, he pondered more about General Lee, recalling some tidbits he had often read:

The man Booker T. Washington, America's foremost Black Educator, noted was the first white person in America to exhibit interest in "saving the soul" of blacks through the medium of the Sunday-school, was born in Virginia in 1807.

Lee's father was a hero of the American Revolution, served as governor of Virginia and as a member of the United States House of Representatives. Members of his family also signed the Declaration of Independence.

Lee was educated in the schools of Alexandria, Virginia, receiving an appointment to the United States Military Academy at West Point at the age of 16. He graduated second in his class, without a single demerit.

Lee was commissioned as 2nd Lieutenant of the United States Engineer Corps. His first assignment was supervising the construction of the now-famous Fort Pulaski, just outside Savannah, Georgia.

Robert's wife, Mary, was the daughter of George Washington Parke Custis, grandson of Martha Washington and adopted son of George Washington. She and Robert raised seven children at Arlington House, which was transferred to the National Park Service in 1933. In 1955, the mansion was designated as a memorial to Robert E. Lee atop Arlington Cemetery, with an inspiring view of the Potomac River and Washington DC.

In 1836, Lee was appointed first Lieutenant, and in 1848, he distinguished himself during the War with Mexico as a Captain.

Lee was appointed superintendent of West Point in 1852, at the tender age of 43.

Less than a decade later, President Abraham Lincoln offered Lee command of the Union Army, but he refused, saying "I cannot raise my hand against my birthplace, my home, my children." That "home" was Virginia, of course.

Isaac had read that Lee wrestled with his soul for days on end regarding this decision. After all, he had faithfully served in the United States Army for over 30 years. A true patriot of a great American state though, Lee reluctantly resigned his commission and headed home to Virginia.

After four brutal years of war, Lee, hardly a warmonger, had learned much. To wit, he stated the famous "It is a good thing war is so terrible; else we should grow too fond of it."

The rest, as they say, is history----and not included in Isaac's museum since his building only told the story of America's 20th Century.

As the Mazda tore down 81, Lexington, Virginia beckoned.

Isaac recalled that in the fall of 1865, months after the Civil War ended, Lee accepted the presidency of troubled Washington College in Lexington. The school was renamed Washington and Lee in his memory after he died of a heart attack five short years later, at the age of 63.

Sir Winston Churchill called this legendary General of the Army of Northern Virginia, "one of the noblest Americans who ever lived." Considering the esteemed source, that's quite the compliment.

In today's age where patriotism and duty is often mocked, Isaac decided he agreed with the quote, and recalled Lee's most famous quote to one of his sons in an 1852 letter: **"Duty is the sublimest word in our language."**

A great American was Robert E. Lee. Of this there was simply no doubt.

And then Mr. Hyde moved further southwest along the spine of the grandest mountain range east of America's great Mississippi River. He knew from past travels, reading, and the types of cars and people he saw along the way, that he was entering "Real South." The mercury, now past 90 degrees, confirmed this supposition, as did perhaps the "Trust Jesus" billboards, though one could also find those in most of rural America. Although Isaac was not overly religious, he could respect that the majority of America, unlike in the urban cities, does not fear Christianity.

About 100 miles or so from the Tennessee state line, and with lamblike clouds overhead and the sun dipping ever so slightly on this late summer evening, Isaac passed the exit for Blacksburg, Virginia, home of Virginia Tech University. It was here, as most recall, that in April 2007, nearly three dozen students and faculty were gunned down by a student's maniacal, premeditated killing spree. With the campus just about ten miles north of the Interstate, Isaac felt an early dinner and stroll in the hills around town might be a decent plan. He was, after all, fewer than four short hours of open road from Knoxville, Tennessee, and the time was only 5:30pm. Isaac had been driving for nearly eight hours and 500 miles, so he was two-thirds of the way to his destination. And he had spent close to half of his 500 miles today in the Commonwealth of Virginia.

In many ways, Blacksburg is a quintessential college town. After exiting a state highway, the university hits you far before the actual city of nearly 40,000 denizens. Actually, Lane Stadium, home of the football team, appears first. Isaac could now understand what it might mean to hear or read that "a town stops when the local squad suits up on a Saturday." The stadium, which frames not only the campus but the town when approaching from the angle Isaac did down a long, well-paved road, holds close to 70,000 fans, and is nearly double the size of Blacksburg. It was reminiscent of Penn State University, situated way up in the central Pennsylvania town of State College, far from Philadelphia or Pittsburgh. Blacksburg's relative isolation from not only the rest of the state added to its appeal, as did its seclusion from the east coast media. Washington DC, at the northern border of Virginia for example, is some 275 miles to the northeast.

On April 16, 2007, however, the world knew all about this town and this public school of nearly more than 22,000 undergrads—but for all the wrong reasons. Always thorough and curious, Isaac went to seek out local insight and reflections upon the tragedy that befell this community when it lost 32 good people to a deranged assassin.

After parking the Mazda in the visitors' lot, a stroll around town did not produce much insight, other than that Blacksburg seemed, as the media reports that fateful day often relayed, to be the perfect college town where anyone would feel safe. Isaac saw a quaint Main Street with a mix of bookstores, coffee shops, sandwich dives and simple locales for townsfolk. Though it appeared the college area ended just outside the university grounds as houses and farmland began to dot the hills in the distance just below the larger mountains, Blacksburg was anything but creepy or dangerous; it seemed like a lovely place to attend school.

At this juncture, Isaac did not have the time nor the need to ruin his relaxed mindset with too much investigative journalism, but he was famished, so he walked back through the main quad---covered on all sides with gray gothic style buildings---and popped into the Student Union. It was fairly crowded, as many students were back preparing for the new semester that also started Monday.

A gregarious young lady asked him for directions to a lecture hall.

"Sorry, I'm just passing by," Isaac said with a smile.

"Ok, uh, I didn't think anyone could really "pass by" Blacksburg," she said back in a friendly way. "It's kinda' like a place you have to seek out."

"Well, you know, with all that went on here last spring, I just wanted to…" Isaac muttered, a bit embarrassed.

"Oh, are you like a journalist or something," she asked.

Isaac suddenly realized he was 45, not 19 or even 24, and felt out of place. He also wondered if he should tell this lady why he was there. Why was he there, after all? Even he did not really know.

"No, well, sort of…but I'm here to look around. Sorry, I don't know where that hall is. Guess I'm the wrong person to ask," he said, and began to walk away.

Then he stopped and asked the girl, "Do you remember that day? What was it like?"

"Oh no, I'm a freshman. I was in high school over in Lynchburg. I'm just starting here," she said. "Otherwise I'd know where I was going."

"I see," Isaac chuckled. "Well, good luck with that. I'm gonna' keep looking around, not like a journalist though."

The co-ed gave Isaac a genuine smile, then turned and walked away.

Isaac harkened back to how carefree and sheltered from the real world college was, and overall, how much he enjoyed the people he met.

Then he realized that, though he was still young-looking and in decent shape, that this girl was in fact just four years older than Lauren. Isaac could have been her father!

With that, he grabbed a turkey sandwich and diet Mountain Dew, ambled through campus for a few more minutes, took a few photos, made some mental notes on the set up, hopped back in the Mazda and headed back to the state highway, knowing he'd have plenty of time to "experience" college again in the coming year.

Interstate 81 at this point---these few hundred miles of mountainous, undulating terrain, within the state of Virginia, then Tennessee's northeastern portion---were smooth and defined "melancholy." The deeper Isaac penetrated into the nation's heart, the greener it became. Everything was lush, and it seemed as though summer had arrived months, not just weeks, ago.

About halfway between Blacksburg and Knoxville came the towns of Bristol, which actually straddle the border of Virginia and Tennessee, thereby existing in both states.

Isaac recalled a story a friend once told him about the big NASCAR races that occur in the Bristol area each year, and how all hotels on 81 throughout Virginia and Tennessee are booked solid. Today, there was little traffic or fanfare as Isaac trekked across the state line whereupon he came across Bristol, Tennessee, Virginia's slightly larger twin. Both cities are under 25,000 in population, but the sign welcoming you does inform passers-by that both Bristols are "a good place to live."

The Great Smoky Mountains, their eponymous National Park, and all the tourist debauchery that is Gatlinburg and Dolly Parton Land (Pigeon Forge, TN.), was off to the southeast of Isaac now. About 20 and 35 miles further southwest, the Mazda passed signs for the two other cities in the "Tri-City" Region of eastern Tennessee: Kingsport and Johnson City.

Stopping to get gas with about two hours of daylight left on a summer evening in the hills of the Volunteer State, Isaac estimated he was 100 miles from the University of Tennessee in Knoxville. That seemed to amount to 90 minutes of driving, barring any traffic or stops, neither of which Isaac expected, as he bought some pretzels and southern sweet tea to tide him over until arrival.

The last portion of the drive was majestic. The sun was dipping, the temperature cooled down a bit so Isaac could finally open the window and enjoy the fresh air rather than recirculated AC, and he could see the hills of Appalachia all around him. Though the area was poorer than most urban American ghettos, it was peaceful at least.

Looking out the window, Isaac longed to take some county or state roads all the way through the green and blue hills and into Knoxville, but by his estimates, maybe two hours of daylight remained as he emerged from the Tri-City Region with more than an hour to the city, so he pressed on. At least I-81 was prettier at this point than most US interstates.

As the sun set to the northwest and Isaac moved southwest, he came upon the Knoxville city limits, whereupon Interstates 81, 26 and 40 meet each other.

Knoxville sits at the western edge of the Smoky Mountain portion of the southern Appalachian mountain range. Most of the campus is nestled in some hills, with the athletic facilities and Tennessee River below. Especially for football games and other events down by the river, it is quite breathtaking. It looks like a smaller, warmer version of Pittsburgh, Pennsylvania.

In the southeast part of the city, the French Broad River (flowing from the hippie hamlet of Asheville in Western North Carolina) joins the Holston River to form the Tennessee.

With a city population of just under 200,000 and a metropolitan populace of over 650,000 people, Knoxville is the third largest city in the Volunteer State, and the state's second oldest to Nashville, which was founded in 1779, though Knoxville was "incorporated" earlier.

Tennessee was admitted into the Union in 1796 and Knoxville was the state's first capital for about 25 years. Then, being that the city was too far east for central location in this very long state, the capital moved to Murfreesboro for eight years. In 1826, Nashville, conveniently sitting in the north central part of the state, became the state capital. The city was named for Francis Nash, a brigadier general killed early in the Revolutionary War.

Knoxville, of course, was named in honor of the first Secretary of War, Henry Knox, who served in that capacity from 1785-1794. He was formerly most famous as the corpulent Massachusetts bookseller who had the preposterous idea of hauling 59 guns from Fort Ticonderoga over the mountains to Boston in the dead of winter in 1775-76 to aid the colonists' cause during the Siege of Boston early in the American Revolution. The intrepid 25 year-old accomplished the feat of hauling these 60 tons of materiel, with the help of 80 yoke of oxen on sleds. In total, the journey was 300 miles over eight weeks, including crossing Lake George, the Hudson River and Berskshire Mountains.

"See what happens when one spends two decades studying one subject?" Isaac muttered to himself amusingly, recalling this from memory, as he looked for the proper exit off I-81 as I-75 and I-40 merged simultaneously.

After locating said exit, Isaac was tired and needed coffee, a good local map, and someone with so-called "southern hospitality" to direct him toward the off-campus condo he had rented for the year.

He came upon what seemed to be Main Street, just past dinner-time and prior to when nightlife might begin. The street was quiet, and the Chamber of Commerce was closed. But alas, there was a city guide pamphlet available outside. Isaac perused it, took in a view of the rivers below, then located where he needed to head, but also some new tidbits. This was exciting to him.

For example, it noted:

"One of Knoxville's nicknames is The Marble City. In the early 20th century a number of quarries were active in the city, supplying Tennessee pink marble (actually Ordovician limestone of the Holston Formation) to much of the country. Notable buildings such as the National Gallery of Art in Washington are constructed of Knoxville marble. The National Gallery's fountains were turned by Candoro Marble Company, which once ran the largest marble lathes in the United States."

With that bit of historic and architectural knowledge now embedded, Isaac consulted the best local map he had. No GPS for him. The world, after all, existed prior to that invention, and he was confident it would continue to do so.

Isaac knew his new abode was no more than a mile from campus, in the first set of hills between the interstate and campus, even farther above the school with a view of the rivers and skyline below. So he proceeded up that way.

As he and the Mazda climbed higher, Isaac stopped at certain points to view the beginnings of the sunset. It was not quite Pittsburgh's awe-inspiring views, but it was very similar. After the sunset, and a deep breath, Isaac felt this was the "right time" to begin his time in Knoxville. He turned the corner and there appeared his domicile.

The term "domicile" came to Isaac's mind since the apartment seemed rather diminutive. But it was, as advertised, on a hill overlooking the campus, city and rivers, which is what Isaac had read and seen on the internet. This was essential to a man such as he. The price was a relief too: easily less than a quarter of what an apartment of this style would rent for in New York City. Overall, Knoxville's media home price was around $100,000 compared to a national average of close to $300,000, much less his home county in New Jersey, which was well over half a million.

At first, Knoxville did not seem quite as bucolic and serene as Isaac had envisioned. Perhaps this was because it was late August, and thus, beastly hot, even as dusk set in. It was also quite humid, though being from New Jersey, Isaac knew a thing or two about that as well. Even summers he spent up in Potsdam often got scorching.

Though Isaac knew Knoxville---often called "Knox Vegas"---had a sizeable population, especially when you include the 38,000 students from all 50 states and 100 countries, he figured that, coming from bigger cities, Knoxville would seem manageable, tidy and peaceful. And it usually was.

But with loud students milling about the main drag in anticipation of the beginning of the fall term, it was anything but on this day. Additionally, some rather blighted areas popped up all around as they do in the south (unlike the north where the "urban" locales are quite segregated from the twee suburbs), and some dilapidated skyscrapers seemed to hang, quite literally in some cases, over the rivers and bridges below. Isaac was discouraged for a few moments. Then he realized he was "a free man," residing in a 215 year old city with great history, museums, scenic vistas on all sides, and less than an hour from Smokey Mountain National Park. He quickly felt better.

Most would have been content to call it a day, move into their new digs, begin unpacking and preparing for the unending errands and administrative matters he or she would need to do in the next 48 hours, leaving any further explorations for another time; but Isaac knew he was weird. On his own volition, despite driving all day, Isaac still fancied another quick drive past the outskirts of town, deep into the Appalachian hills. He also knew he had time, though the sun was setting rapidly; therefore the journey would be a quick one.

Isaac prodded off eastward on the highway, past the outskirts of town, and some real rural southern poverty that is typical of the south, past the minor league baseball stadium and into some rolling hills. He enjoyed getting the lay of the land as well as some important landmarks. When darkness set in, and Isaac noted a sign declaring Smoky Mountain Park 45 miles further along the twisty state highway, he called it a day and headed back, leaving all this for another time. Many other times, he hoped.

After a weekend of furniture, grocery and class shopping, the school year began rather mundanely. As a forty-something, though he admired the youthful exuberance of college life, he also was reticent to embrace it. Isaac knew the eventual pitfalls of so much of it, and saw through the banality of it all as someone who had seen the real world for the past two decades. After all, he had graduated from Clarkson before nearly any of these children were alive.

These "kids" just seemed so narcissistic and materialistic, not to mention self-righteous, but in the most transparent way. Nearly every discussion Isaac overheard was about Facebook, and the word "like" was used incessantly. And this was in the Bible Belt, not the coasts or Chicago, where it would be undoubtedly worse. But while Isaac saw this behavior during his days on campus and occasionally at restaurants, he had purposely picked an area that was occupied mostly by adults, even some professors, but very few students. It was quiet and perfect.

Academically, the year was a breeze to start. Isaac had hoped and frankly assumed it would be. Though this was a Masters course with a small class-size and thus the intricate attention of his instructor, most of the 12-15 other students in his three classes were recent graduates who had, as Isaac mused silently and on the phone to Ana, "never worked a day in their lives." Now, the students at UT-Knoxville were mostly from this region of the country, and this being a public school, they were certainly not all wealthy, snooty or privileged as you'd be more likely to find in Southern California or the Northeast, but they were still naïve, almost to the point of sorrow. Isaac also knew he was this way when he was 23 as well, or at least he guessed he was, even though he was already working at the museum by then.

Most of the classes had men, but there were some women, often the southern blonde types who were interested in Isaac's story in terms of why he was in eastern Tennessee. They often flirted innocently with him, but knew he was married and certainly had no ill intentions. The guys were mostly studious but also invited Isaac out drinking often, to which he normally declined. His one "vice" was the football games down at Neyland Stadium every other Saturday night. Neyland, seating over 100,000 mostly drunken Appalachian fans, was a classic facility. This was an event not to be missed, and Isaac, donning his Orange Peyton Manning jersey he bought at the bookstore the first day of classes, hung out with the students and acted like a college kid…for about 200 minutes each week. He rarely went out afterwards to celebrate wins or drink the loss away. By September's end though, Tennessee football had begun a rough year by their lofty standards, in which the team was 2-2, already suffering a home loss to archrival Florida.

In mid-October, Isaac began to miss the change of leaves which, though it would occur at some point, did not come when Isaac was used to it in the northeast. He had visited the Smokies on a hot September day and a balmy October day and, though it was serene, green and spectacular, had not a hint of evidence that summer was ending. The campus looked much as it did six weeks back, when he arrived. This was not Florida, but it was still the South, so most students still wore t-shirts shorts into November, despite the global decrease in temperatures the past decade.

Isaac, though he swore he would avoid the "college scene," had been invited out a few times by some of his classmates, and had met some surprisingly mature grad students as well as undergrads. He seemed to serve as a father (or older brother) figure to many of the 20-somethings. One lady quickly plucked Isaac as her personal psychologist, it seemed, when he chatted with her a few times at a local sandwich shoppe.

Isaac did not go out much, other than to do some sightseeing or visit the occasional historical center, but at those places he rarely ran into classmates or UT students. But at the food places in town, fellow students were unavoidable. This is where Isaac met Becky.

Becky was unremarkable in her appearance, neither pretty nor homely, just simple. And though she occasionally seemed a bit naïve, coming from a small town to the south of Knoxville, and the first in her family to attend an institute of higher learning, she also was very astute when it came to worldly matters. Becky had a brain that was constantly moving and Isaac admired that. Many of the uppity northeastern girls and women he and Ana knew would not been keen on Becky because her parents weren't college educated, nor neurotic. Instead, they were happy folks, preferring sports, family and church. Isaac enjoyed this change.

Isaac and Becky chatted eruditely on various matters and while Isaac talked about New York City (where Becky had never been, *nor wanted to visit*, which was intriguing in and of itself), Becky talked about the Appalachian hills, farms, chores, and her family's houseboat that they rented and lived on for many summers past.

Though she did not know many Jewish people, she understood and admired Judaism far more than many Jewish girls Isaac knew. In that sense, she reminded him of Ana's vast knowledge on a religion that was not even hers. And thankfully, when the topic became too personal, not only did Becky know Isaac was married, and more than two decades her senior, but she also had a serious boyfriend she'd dated since high school. He worked for John Deere back in her hometown as a technician and helped her financially as best he could. Becky often went home on weekends, and this Travis fellow did not seem to mind that Isaac was a nice friend she had met. It actually made Travis more comfortable, since she had an older, mature male companion to advise and protect her.

In fact, due to their propinquity of societal views, Isaac and Travis hit it off right away. Travis had done two tours in Iraq during the Global War on Terror, and Isaac found his tales fascinating and far different from the doom and gloom the media publicized. Travis would meet Isaac every so often for coffee, as he preferred to stay away from campus for his own sanity. As a veteran, he truly was angered by all the collegians donning "Peace" shirts to make fashion or political statement, as well as the "anti-war" rallies and much else.

"You know who really is desperate for peace? The Iraqis, the Afghanis, the Muslim women, and especially those of us fighting to bring that to them," he would often tell Isaac. "I hate war, man. Only a solider who's seen war first hand can honestly say they hate war. But I will always fight for folks' freedom to do and say as they see fit."

Isaac immediately told Travis that General Dwight D. Eisenhower began a famous 1946 speech with those very words. He added that this rhetoric of "fighting" for someone's liberty and self-determination was a lot more plausible coming from a soldier, than the hollow words of some civil rights lawyer talking about "protecting" someone's First Amendment right, when there was never action behind the platitudes.

Isaac also told Travis, "It's unfortunate that the best way to secure peace is often to by preparing for war." It was a quote from John F. Kennedy. Travis seemed shocked that a Democrat president has spoken in such hawkish terms, considering the current modus operandi of the Statists running the Democrat Party in the 21st century. Isaac, not ready for history lessons, simply noted that "my father's Democrat party bears little resemblance to today's." Travis understood completely, his father, like Isaac's, having been a Truman Democrat, disaffected in the 60s, that moved right on the political spectrum over time.

A week later, Travis had the JFK quote about "securing peace" through war on his Facebook page. Okay, so seemingly everyone did have one of those accounts, Isaac confessed to Ana one night on the phone.

Days and weeks went by and the two of them saw each other sporadically, but otherwise, Isaac studied and aced most of his papers, presentations and exams. His Masters would eventually be a dual Masters that "UTK" offered in Military History and "Developmental Leadership," which was some newfangled program Isaac normally would snicker at, but it sounded so perfect for his job back home that he did not care. Isaac just wanted to do what he was there for, as though it was a mission, then "withdraw" back to the northeast.

Then, on the night of the final football game in mid-November, just a week before Isaac was going to head home for Thanksgiving, matters in Marble City changed.

7

Lauren, Ana, and especially Ross, were longing to see their father. Ross and Isaac were never able to meet up during the fall, nor had Ana been inclined for a weekend sojourn, so all were eager for a Turkey Day reunion and the extended weekend. Lauren, who had not dated any boys this school year as part of a promise to her father, even showed great interest in seeing the man she once affectionately called "dada."

The Saturday night that preceded Thanksgiving was the Vols final home football game as well as their final game of the season. The team now eight wins against three losses, were in a position to post a 9th win and make it to a good Bowl Game. Tennessee was hosting border rival Kentucky, who was having a stellar season, also at eight up, three down. Isaac was very excited for the 7:30pm kickoff, and planned to grab dinner prior to the game with Becky and Travis at a local Chinese food place.

Having finished all the writing he had to do for school throughout the day, Isaac was in a great mood. Not only was he heading home soon, but he had planned a day-trip to the Smokies "and beyond" for Sunday, whereupon he planned to explore other parts of Western North Carolina. Then he'd have two easy days of classes before going to see his family.

Becky and Travis were very late arriving for a bite to eat. They'all had planned for 6pm, and unlike most girls Isaac knew back home, Becky was punctual. At 6:20 or so, Isaac called her and Travis answered.

"Hey buddy, uh, I don't think we'll make dinner," Travis said in a rush, as opposed to his usual Appalachian drawl. "We should be at the game, just a tad late."

Rather than pry deeper, since this was Travis and not Becky, therefore Isaac did not feel comfortable playing amateur psychologist, he quickly asked, "Everything all right, man?"

"Sort of. Not totally, but no worries." Travis said.

Isaac knew something was awry. He daringly asked if Becky wanted to speak with him, and instead of Travis perhaps being offended, he gave her the phone.

"What's up?" Isaac asked, purposely in as benign a tone as possible.

Never one to feel sorry for herself, Becky was blunt.

"I'm pregnant," she said matter-of-factly.

Isaac's first thought was how pleasant it was not to hear a woman say "we're pregnant" since in fact only one person can be pregnant, but then the facts hit him, and he was silent.

Then he muttered the cliché, "Are you sure?" to which Becky affirmed.

"Well, congratulations!" Isaac shouted, hoping that this was something the unmarried couple at least was somewhat happy about.

Becky thanked him, but clearly she was befuddled. She was 22, the same age her mother was when she had Becky, but Becky was living a different life so far. She was an educated woman, striving for a white-collar career. Her mother had married her father at age 19, and led a loving life as a homemaker and mom of five.

One thing Isaac knew, with Becky being a religious southerner girl, was that abortion was never going to be an option. He may have been something of a secular Jew, but with Ana's wisdom, common sense and his perspicacity, he knew the murder of nascent life was completely immoral.

As he queried Becky about the possibility of an abortion, she was silent. Isaac pressed again, asking her to recall her upbringing, mainly morals versus convenience. Becky was still silent. Then Travis got on the line.

"Hey, listen we'll talk to you'all later…"

Isaac thought of interjecting, but decided to let it go by the wayside for now, realizing neither of them was in a frame of rational mind for sentient discourse on this important matter. Isaac later realized he has gone way too far into Becky's personal matters. She and Travis didn't show up to the game at all, Tennessee lost, and Isaac didn't enjoy the game one bit.

A long day later, after not hearing from Becky, Isaac pondered a further intervention, but decided against it, as he did not want to seem pushy nor conceited, especially as an "outsider." Growing up, Isaac's family was tacitly "pro-choice," though they still saw the immorality in abortions.

But still, this was inapposite to Ana's family of Catholics who were vehemently pro-life. These folks had shown Isaac how inhumane the murder of the "most vulnerable among us" is. They cited telling statistics about the very high percentage of abortions that occur "out of convenience" – not uneducated kids in penury -- by couples in their late twenties who are more than ready to have children, but instead put their lives before that of a nascent being.

All these facts, rather than emotion, made an impression upon Isaac, leading him to rectify prior uninformed conjectures. Though when he tried to impart some newfound wisdom to friends and family, Isaac was often met with disbelief. He knew these folks had never thought deeply about right and wrong, yet still had heard him, and would perhaps ponder someday.

One night Isaac came over to Becky's to learn of her decision, which was to keep the baby. Isaac felt mostly relieved. He, Becky and Travis had a good talk about responsibility, morals and common sense---all of which Isaac believed they had utilized in making this "progressive' decision. Isaac left their place in a good mood that chilly Knoxville night.

Until he arrived back at his apartment.

Upon entering, Isaac noticed his cell phone, which he had mistakenly left on the counter a few hours back when he'd departed, had 21 missed calls, but no voice mails. All but one of the calls was from Ana. In all their years of marriage, though Ana could be persistent and needy at times, she had never called that many times in an evening.

Isaac dialed his familiar home phone number.

Ross answered. He sounded excited to speak to his dad, yet full of angst.

"Hey, champ, how are things?" Isaac inquired nervously, as he still felt a twinge of guilt by not being around Ross as a father figure the past few months.

"Good, I'll put mom on." He was quick and curt. Isaac braced for the worse.

"Isaac, we need to talk," Ana demanded.

Isaac wanted to sarcastically say, "That's clear from the 20 plus calls," but instead he muttered, "Okay, is something wrong?"

Ana was rather forward. "Yes, very much so."

Isaac wondered if this was serious, or about his not being around, which had come up every so often the past few months; but since he was days away from seeing them, Isaac was caught off guard by the tone on the other end.

"When do you get home?" Ana asked.

Isaac informed her, in a kind way, that while he could not predict the exact time, it would likely be late Wednesday night, and then he'd spend three full days at home before heading back first thing Sunday morning. He hoped his family would appreciate that he was making the incredibly long drive up in one day, but realized this was not the time to draw attention to that.

Ana continued, "Okay, we can talk about it then."

Isaac was frustrated, and pressed to know more. Ana relented only a bit.

"No, it's nothing urgent," she sniffed and sounded choked up. "It's just tough here, and we all miss you."

Now Isaac, for the first time since departing in August, felt sad. But rather than give in, he made a simple declaration.

"I understand completely," he rightly admitted. "I miss you too. So tell the kids I will be home really soon---like way less than a week. Basically half a week, okay?"

Ana affirmed. Isaac knew if it was truly urgent, Ana would have said so.

With all that on his mind, and though he had just ventured out for a day's hike and drive into the Smokies on Sunday, Isaac planned another short sojourn for Tuesday. He figured he was already missing class Wednesday, so he'd take Tuesday off. His work done, Isaac informed one of his instructors and was off mid-morning after a good night's sleep. He was not headed directly home, but instead was planning a slight detour after leaving the Knoxville Metro Area. His target: mountainous and gorgeous Cumberland Gap National Historic Park, a mere 60 miles north of Knoxville.

Isaac had always wanted to visit this historic and scenic spot, but its location in the "gap" of the largest portion of the Appalachian Mountains, as well as massive distance from most interstates, had precluded him. The "detour" from Knoxville on the way back home was not severe enough to cost him more than an hour or two, so on Tuesday morning, he packed about a week's worth of clothing into the Mazda and headed back to northern New Jersey, via the tri-border of Virginia, Tennessee and Kentucky.

8

The appeal of Cumberland Gap combined Isaac's two favorite types of park: history and majestic scenery.

The drive on a cool, but calm day, took no more than 90 minutes up windy State Highway 33, until Isaac crossed into Middlesboro, Kentucky. The park entrance was just outside town, free, and easy to navigate.

On a 45 degree sunny day at base, Isaac drove up a four mile twisty hill to an area of the Park called "Pinnacle Overlook." As the Mazda rose in a steep, circular pattern around the backbone of the mountain, snow and deer could be spotted as the elevation increased dramatically from roughly 1600 feet to nearly 3000 feet.

After parking and walking about 200 yards to the zenith, all the day's driving was well worth the time. Incredible, diverse views of three American states at sunset quickly presented themselves.

More than a half mile up in the air, its history was easy for Mr. Hyde to recall:

More than three hundred thousand settlers crossed this brutal and narrow gap---the chief passageway in the "middle" of the immense Appalachians---in the late 18th and early 19th centuries on their way to Kentucky, as well as the lands of the Northwest Territory and Ohio Valley. The famous pioneer Daniel Boone led a company of men to widen the path through the gap to make settlement along the Kentucky and Tennessee frontiers easier in 1775. The trail was again widened in the 1790s to accommodate wagon traffic. Today, according to a notice in the visitors' center, nearly 20,000 cars pass beneath the site daily via the Tunnel built in 1996, and 1.2 million people visit the park annually.

The "gap" was formed by an ancient creek, flowing southward, which cut through the land being pushed up to form the mountains.

Like many parts of the American colonies, the Gap was named for a Briton: Prince William Augustus, Duke of Cumberland. The explorer Thomas Walker, who has historic sites in the Park and throughout the region, also gave the surname to the Cumberland River in 1750, and the name soon spread to many other features in the region.

Isaac looked down once he was at the very top, noticing Middlesboro, Kentucky, a sizeable town of just under 13,000 folks to the northwest, and Historic Cumberland Gap, Tennessee, was dead center, 2,000 feet directly below, nestled in charming hills. The Cumberland River, snaking its way southwest through undulating autumnal hills toward Middle Tennessee, was beyond that and easily visible---with the Smokey Mountains off to the due south about 80 or so miles. About eight steps to the left of the scenic viewing area, was a great shot of the extreme southwest corner of Virginia and Powell's Valley with the southern terminus of the Blue Ridge Mountains far in the distance. Tranquil lakes, so smooth and shiny they might be scenes painted on a glass plate, were visible on all sides.

Though looking down at the Virginia, Isaac was standing more than 500 miles from Virginia Beach and any oceanfront property in the Commonwealth. Isaac was also closer to the Mississippi River in Cairo, Illinois, than the Atlantic Ocean. And while he was nearly as far west as Cincinnati, Isaac also was just a poke under 460 miles from the Nation's Capital. Clearly, Virginia is an enormous state with an equally enormous history. And to think that for more than 250 of its 400 year existence, present-day West Virginia, another of America's scenic and historic treasures, was part of the same state. Tennessee, on the other hand, with an equally impressive history, was second only to Virginia in troops supplied to the Confederacy during the Civil War, and the Gap played a key strategic role during the War Between the States.

As the sun dipped just a bit on this late November afternoon, Isaac took a cursory visit to the historic town of Cumberland Gap, Tennessee on the other side of the pristine tunnel. There he read a local brochure in this well kept, quaint town. It appeared that part of the Rebel effort in East Tennessee involved controlling this Gap's thoroughfare. From whom? Fellow Tennesseans, as scores of Union sympathizers, too far from the southern agricultural and cotton economy to benefit monetarily, resided in the Appalachian hills. Difficult to defend, the Confederates regarded the Cumberland Gap as a gateway to the region and seized it early in the war. Indeed this area was so precarious for the Rebels that the *Confederacy* has to construct strategic forts all throughout the region to maintain some sort of aegis. These lines of defense collapsed in the spring of 1862 after Confederate Brigadier General Felix Zollicoffer was killed at a battle at the nearby Fishers Creek. He was the first Confederate General killed in the war's Western Theater. No other campaigns occurred in the Gap's vicinity thereafter.

And with that, Isaac, satisfied, was off. It was cold out. So he headed north? Familial obligations awaited.

There was simply no way Isaac could drive the 700 miles this afternoon and evening. Thus he plowed his way back to Interstate 81, which took nearly two hours, and settled in for the evening at a Sleep Inn in Dublin, Virginia. That would leave an even 500 miles for his ride home Wednesday, meaning Isaac would still return by dinner time Wednesday, and surely in plenty of time to prepare for the great Thanksgiving feast Thursday afternoon.

Having driven this same entire route three months prior, though he enjoyed the scenery in a different season, Isaac roared along northeast, only stopping for gas and lunch. After leaving the hotel in the hills of southwestern Virginia at 0800 hours, he pulled into the family driveway, to the cheers and hugs of his family, prior to 1600 hours. It was good to be home.

9

Being home was soothing for Isaac, mostly. There were no major arguments over the holiday weekend, just discussions. No one begged him to leave school and come home early, just inquired as to how things were going---as if the family did not already talk daily.

But Isaac sensed not all was copasetic. Ross was a bit distant and downcast, while Lauren seemed itching to see her friends, and lacking a driver's license, was prodding her parents at every chance to "go out" even though it was explained to her that dad was only here for a few days and she'd have plenty of other times to hang out with friends. Telling that to a ninth grade girl seemed easier said than enacted.

As for those urgent "issues," it appeared to Isaac that when Ana had called him a few days ago, she had been emotional, perhaps caught up in the moment, and confused as to why his phone was off. Isaac never broached the subject of what was specifically irking Ana, and she did not offer an explanation. But overall, events transpired as swimmingly as Isaac could have desired, until departure on Sunday morning.

Lauren had been permitted to go out the prior night and the rest of the Hyde clan had an early dinner, then watched sports and a movie on television. When Lauren did not call for a pick-up by 11, as promised, Isaac called her. After she begged for another hour out and Isaac said no, explaining why, she begrudgingly accepted the decision, even after some terse words that Isaac mostly ignored. He did not want to sound didactic, but he was the dad.

The "compromise," which Isaac knew was not a brilliant idea but sought in order to avoid fighting, was that her friend could stay over at the Hyde house that night, as long as Lauren rose by 9am to say good-bye to dad.

Up early the following morning, Isaac went for a walk with Ross, talked sports, school and so on, apologized profusely for his extended absence but promised he'd return soon for the holidays. Isaac told his son that spring would zip by, and when dad returned, Ross would get a big gift and life would improve dramatically. To a ten year-old, that worked well.

Lauren was not so easy, because upon entering the bedroom, she and her friend were nowhere to be found. The Hydes were baffled, but at around 9:10am, Lauren appeared alone.

"I went to walk Shannon home, ok?" she said angrily.

"Sure," Isaac said. "But you did not ask, and that attitude isn't really necessary, is it?"

"Whatever," she said and gave Isaac a half-hearted hug, then muttered, "See you soon, I guess."

Isaac was not about to push the envelope, but Ana, who obviously had dealt with this attitude for many months, was.

"Even if I ignore how rude you were to your father, you need to ask when you leave the house early in the morning," mom said firmly. "Otherwise, I'll assume you sneaked out in the middle of the night."

"Ok, but of course, I did not sneak out," Lauren said. "That would be stupid."

"So is going out in the morning," Ross said with a laugh.

Isaac ushered him inside.

"Lauren, exactly why did you need to walk Shannon home?" Ana asked.

Lauren was taken aback. She told her parents that Shannon had not felt well, which, though likely a white lie, appeased them, especially Isaac, who was itching to depart.

"Ok, well, be careful," Isaac said. He hugged her again, noticing an odd smell – perhaps alcohol -- then bid farewell to Ross and Ana. He noted to his wife that Lauren needed to be very careful, especially with distractions like boys, girlfriends and other unsavory activities. Isaac recommended Lauren go out for the tennis team in the spring, which would keep her out of trouble, as sports tend to do for teenage girls, much like Ana back in Indiana as a youth. Ana concurred.

Isaac departed on this sun-soaked, balmy winter morning, still pondering Lauren's "adult" behavior.

He then thought of Becky.

Becky came into his mind due to Isaac's recent situation with Lauren. Like Lauren, Becky was undoubtedly a wholesome girl. But she was also different. Having a child out of wedlock notwithstanding, Becky seemed responsible, overall. Lauren, at least at her current age, did not. But if Lauren found herself in Becky's predicament five or so years down life's road, what would she do about an "unexpected" child? And moreover, if Becky had been in Lauren's situation five years ago, experimenting with how far to push her parents, where did she stop? If nothing else, Isaac longed to use Becky as an example for Lauren, especially since he saw her often and felt there were at least some working similarities, despite very different upbringings.

Isaac's bachelors' degree surely was not in Psychology, but Ana's was. So he decided to call her....later on into the drive. For now, he let his mind go, put on some football on the radio, and allowed his mind to rest---for once.

An hour later, Isaac called Becky and Travis to check in on the goings-on down in Knoxville, his adopted home for the year.

Becky answered quickly, and out of breath, as Isaac rolled thru the hills of Pennsylvania on a much colder (and now bleaker) day than he observed in this direction three months prior.

After asking how things were, Isaac pondered whether he should be dauntless enough to truly ask Becky how the pregnancy was going; was she one hundred percent going to keep the unborn baby; could she give him any "female" advice on what was going on with Lauren, or even his wife?

But he did not. At least not right away.

The two chatted amicably about generic topics, local school gossip, what Isaac had seen on the road and where he was now---since Becky's life travels had been somewhat limited---and when he'd return. They made dinner plans with Travis for the following weekend before finals. Then Isaac inquired about more pressing details.

He was quite relieved to learn Becky, a southern woman of principle, was still keeping the baby. Her parents would help out as best they could, especially to be certain Becky could remain a full time student as long as possible. She also told Isaac that Travis was not only totally "on board" with all the plans, but "very excited about all the upcoming baby/pregnancy stuff." Isaac didn't ask further details about those happenings, though.

Then Isaac, instead of asking personal questions about his family to Becky then and there, told Becky he'd like to get some "female insight" into his teenage daughter's mind, when she had a moment. Knowing she was Isaac's only young female friend (Isaac had considered his mother, but quickly thought better), Becky happily obliged.

Becky seemed perplexed by some of Isaac's quandaries, so much so that he got frustrated repeating some of them to her over coffee cake and orange juice a few days after he returned to Knoxville.

But eventually, she understood and offered some advice.

"Isaac, do you realize that when you're 14, your friends are the most important people in your life?" Becky asked rhetorically. "They define who you are, and how you act depends on how your friends react to those actions."

Isaac squirmed uncomfortably in his chair and dabbed at the cake in front of him, as Becky continued.

"Being accepted by your peers seems like the most important thing in the world. And being excluded can make a girl feel like the world is coming to an end. However, and I know this all sounds cliché, but confiding in your parents, listening to them and spending time with them is not "cool" at all." Becky said, looking up, as if she was recalling her and her parents' relationships.

"But remember always, they are secretly yearning for your guidance and to know that you love and respect them. The trick, and I am no psychologist either, is figuring out how to accomplish this without them actually knowing you're doing it," Becky noted with a smile, sounding anything but supercilious.

Isaac had heard lines like this from Ana many times, but not in such simple terms. Plus, he enjoyed having it "confirmed," so to speak, by someone who had gone through such travails far more recently. It was also good to hear this from a person, not a psychologist.

The historian in Isaac found it humorous to hear that "being excluded" was like "the end of the world." He wondered how the one million seven hundred twenty thousand Soviets, Germans, Romanians, Italians and Hungarians killed during the 161 days of Operation Barbarossa in 1941, or the 1.2 million dead British, French and Germans following the four and a half month Somme Offensive in 1916 would feel about Lauren's "world." But he laughed those off as bad analogies; this was his daughter after all.

Neither Isaac nor Becky had an abundance of time to chat, catch up, or show more concern since finals began in less than a week. Isaac stepped out into the chilliest Appalachian air he'd yet felt on that early December afternoon.

Isaac felt good. Yep, he did. Too chilly and gloomy to hike or go for a drive, he went home and cuddled up with a non-academic book, a cup of coffee and tried to put together a fire in his small fireplace. Either way, he felt some "closure" and was content for the first time in many weeks, even months.

10

Finals, as most of the academic year had been for the 45 year old Isaac, were a formality. He knew the topics, and when the professors, unlike those he had studied under before some of his classmates were born, were giving "hints" and asking for little more than regurgitation of historical occurrences through much of the course, exams were rudimentary. Isaac scored nearly perfect on them, especially in the essay portion. He knew how to write, for he was educated prior to the so-called "dumbing down" of college curriculum that began in the early 90s and continued today, even in a Masters program at a major university.

Wrapping up the fall semester was, as these things often are, bittersweet. Isaac longed to continue his friendship and discussions with Becky – which he'd do, of course, come January – and track her pregnancy as it progressed, but he also looked forward to extended time on the homefront.

Aside from the days in late November, he'd been away for nearly four months. This was longer than Isaac had ever gone without seeing his children. He knew they could not have grown up too much during the fall, but also knew each day was meant to be precious. Isaac had catching up to do – with Ana as well, and she'd surely let him know that.

Doing the same lengthy drive as he did a few weeks back, Isaac pounded the road in furious fashion to get home as quickly as possible. He always poked fun at folks who never stopped to see the sites. He refused to become, as Abigail Adams once called husband and President John, an "inactive spectator," but he had seen many of the spots; it was also cold, and he wanted to see his family. Isaac figured the "G-ds of travel" would understand, and it was likely he'd take some sightseeing detours on the way back down in January. Knoxville to his home in Northern New Jersey was do-able in one long day, and since the weather was cold and clear, this seemed the time to try.

Being one of the shortest days of the year, darkness set in by the time Isaac reached the Virginia suburbs southwest of Washington DC. Isaac had avoided the hills of West Virginia and Pennsylvania due to some slick ice from a recent storm, and had instead cut through the hills on Highway 66 at Winchester and now headed down into the Potomac Valley.

Reaching the DC outskirts at such a late hour, Isaac did not take the 495 Beltway and instead pounded pavement right through Washington DC. The capitol building, the monument and the memorials were glistening off the Potomac and Tidal Basin, with precious few people out on a cold night. Isaac got misty-eyed, realizing as he often did, how proud and lucky he was to live in America.

As he moved through The District and into Maryland, though it was bleak and cold, Isaac also realized how much he missed winter. It may have sounded odd, but with snow on the sides on the road from a recent dump, and protected by the heat of his car and little traffic, this over-crowded region of the eastern seaboard, for a moment, actually seemed serene. The grass is always greener, Isaac mused, as he hit I-95 toward Baltimore and the home stretch, his car's headlights making two melon-colored tunnels along the desolate interstate.

At a few ticks before midnight, after over 11 hours on the road and just one stop, Isaac Hyde arrived home, greeted by warm hugs from all members of his family. Lauren, of all people, still wide awake, seemed especially happy to see "daddy." Entering his clean and familiar home again, Isaac was content and overjoyed.

But why were the kiddies so giddy? And should Isaac have wondered this, or just accepted that his children, after all, were ecstatic to see their papa? He decided on a little of both in his mind and settled in for a cup of tea, a quick chat and bed with his wife.

11

The giddiness of the children and the camaraderie enjoyed by the Hyde family over the next few days was genuine, for sure. Isaac was euphoric to be home. He slept well, ate well, exercised, and saw friends he had not seen in months.

A little over a week after his return – just two days before Christmas and on the actual first night of Chanukkah – the Hydes loaded into the "family vehicle" and drove a few hundred miles west to meet up with the Mendez clan, including Ana's younger brother, Kevin. They had been debating whether to not only make the sojourn, but then afterwards, where to meet up since a full 700 mile trip to Central Indiana did not appeal very much to Isaac after all his recent driving. The decision was the city of Pittsburgh, Pennsylvania, which was slightly more equidistant than Cleveland, Ohio, the other option.

Isaac loved Pittsburgh. He loved its scenery, its history, admired its blue collar mentality and just its "feel." All criteria considered, it was probably his favorite American city. And since the kids and Ana's parents had never visited, though he was tired, Isaac sought to play tour guide as much as possible. Ana, having been to the Steel City with Isaac numerous times over the years, actually vouched for Isaac's knowledge to her parents. Usually she'd poke fun at him, but this time, knowing his desires, she "played along" honestly.

Everyone enjoyed three glorious days in a city whose beauty is unknown to many Americans. They ate fine dinners, stayed at posh hotels with views of water and hills, toured museums, and strolled along the chilly Ohio River. All reveled in the history of this area that goes back to its pre-Revolutionary days, and digested some of the best panoramas in Urban America from the adjacent Mount Washington and surrounding incline railways.

The trip ended with an evening scurrying through Point State Park, which sits at the "pointed" end of the main downtown area, replete with a majestic geyser. It offers a panoramic view of the confluence of the Ohio and Allegheny Rivers. The western view shows the Ohio's snake-like format as it disappears toward Northern West Virginia and Ohio. The Carnegie Science Center, PNC (baseball) Park and Heinz (football) Field are directly in view. Everyone found it quite inspiring and romantic.

Isaac began explaining to the family that most folks' prior knowledge of Pittsburgh had been from what they recalled of the "Steel City" in the 1970s and 1980s: "ugly, smokestacks, bleak, or worse..." But those folks, Isaac claimed, "had never been recently, for certain." Isaac continued, "The only two people I know who had been in the recent past gave a180 degree different description: "awesome, cool, unique, picturesque."

Isaac, though not a Pittsburghian, boasted that Rand McNally labeled Pittsburgh as America's most livable city in 1985 and 2007. And Pittsburgh continues to rank high in quality-of-life comparisons for schools, hospitals and cost of living.

He continued:

"While I wouldn't put this erstwhile mining, smokestack-laden town along the same lines of "Renaissance" as Florence or Madrid, there is little doubt that Pittsburgh would be nearly unrecognizable to someone who had not visited since as recently as the Clinton Administration."

And he closed, as his listeners laughed and shuffled in the flurries that had begun to fall:

"Any discussion of Pittsburgh should recall what the city has always had: a visually striking location, divided by three rivers and countless bridges, surrounded by hills, including, as we saw, Mount Washington, "he said as others repeated with him. "Pittsburgh is the only city in America with an entrance," referring to the Fort Pitt Tunnel, "you come out of it, and bam, the city just smacks you right in the face," he ended, to the sarcastic clapping of his family.

"Son, the Pittsburgh Chamber of Commerce should add you to its payroll," Mauricio told Isaac, as Mr. Hyde stepped down from his fictitious dais. "My friend, I'm sure as a journalist of yesteryear, your dad would've appreciated that."

Chuckling, Isaac realized David most certainly would. After so much time away, it was good to be around family for an extended period.

Upon returning from the rendezvous with the in-laws in Pittsburgh, Isaac still had two glorious weeks remaining at home, and he wanted to refrain, partially upon Ana's request, from any schedules or "inflexible" plans. But he wanted to take the kids to New York City to skate at Rockefeller Centre, and see the holiday sales and lights, journey to the Delaware Water Gap or to the Adirondacks upstate or go to some of their favorite old hangouts and restaurants. Ana had to remind Isaac, as did Lauren and Ross, that he'd be back for good in just a few months. It was not as though they were moving or he was getting divorced. Isaac laughed in agreement each and every time a similar conversation came up. Nonetheless, these were special days for obvious reasons, and all understood their significance, especially as New Years rolled around and Isaac's departure date came closer.

A pleasant New Years' Eve – most importantly with Lauren seeing some friends but returning before the Times Square ball dropped -- was enjoyed by just the four Hydes, as Isaac would be leaving fewer than 36 hours later. They reminisced, planned for a potential spring meet-up, since Isaac would otherwise not be home until late March, and just relaxed and celebrated another year gone by, and a "different one" at that.

"Dad, can we meet in Morgantown like you once promised," Ross asked.

Isaac had tried to arrange such a trip in late October during the brilliant fall foliage season, but it never transpired.

"I hope so, son," Isaac replied. "And maybe the girls will come too."

Ana rolled her eyes in a condescending way, though Lauren, who was suddenly as perky as when she was ten said, "Yeah, that'd be cool. It's a college town, right," she asked, with a wry smile and her eyes ablaze.

"Yes, but that's not why we'd meet there," Isaac half-lied. Even if hedonistic and often overbearing, since he now lived in one, the excitement of a college place like Morgantown, along with its scenery, was similar to Knoxville, so he did look forward to that as well.

"Oh, ok," Lauren relented. "But Jocelyn's brother is a freshman there and he's rushing…"

"He plays football?" Ross piped in.

"Uh, not really…" Lauren smiled, looking at her parents for what to say next.

"Well, I doubt we'd have time to see him," Ana declared, changing the subject, realizing she had three and a half more years of this ordeal before college even began.

That was the end of that tit for tat. A decision would have to be made another time. Isaac paused, acknowledging that Lauren was in fact nearly 15, and that peppy, innocent ten year old was not coming back soon. She was in 9th grade and, aside from her cell phone and learner's permit, cared about one thing: boys. At least it was not going to be "men" on Isaac's watch though.

A few short days later, déjà vu reared its ugly head again. Though this would the penultimate time Isaac would have to do this hello/good-bye visit, the episode truly tore him up inside, and outside, he wasn't much better. So Isaac gave his perfunctory hugs and kisses, pissed that this was happening again, then bolted off down the familiar road west, then south -- arriving, without detours, very late that night in the crisp but pleasant Eastern Tennessee air.

12

A few weeks after he returned to campus, Isaac sensed something was adrift at home due to the tone of Ana's phone calls. She seemed not only distant, but flustered and ruffled. What was going on, Isaac wondered, even asked, but Ana always said "nothing major." He knew otherwise. Ana didn't usually speak so curtly; something was eating at her back in New Jersey. Since she would not share the source of her stress, Isaac could only muse.

His first two inclinations were Lauren or financial matters. If it were Lauren though, Ana would have told him, so Isaac knew it had to be money. However, Ana would need to be specific for him to help; she wasn't at first. Then Isaac simply asked her if it was financial. Ana said it was, then elaborated:

"Isaac, yes honey, it is about money, but it's also compounded by Lauren," she said.

"Again?" Isaac asked, concerned. This he did not expect.

"That's just part of it," Ana added. "It makes things more frustrating."

When Isaac inquired specifically about Lauren, Ana would only say it was "the same things," so Isaac stopped pressing, understanding that Ana was not going to spill any more information. The financial issues were unexpected, thus Isaac asked about those. Ana was hesitant.

"Just the usual bills," she said.

Isaac knew better, then asked her if there was anything more specific over which she was worried.

"Isaac, it's tough right now," she confessed. "We've lost your income, and our expenses are the same, if not more."

He then asked what she thought the best solution was, in the short term, of course.

Ana was silent, then offered a cliché answer about "saving" and "being smart with finances."

Becky called Isaac on the other line at this point, but Isaac wisely ignored her. Ana kept talking. Two minutes later, Becky called again, as Ana continued to rant. Isaac decided to risk it, telling Ana that Becky was calling and it might be an emergency. Ana didn't seem to hear and continued, so Isaac clicked over.

Thankfully, Becky just wanted "to talk." This was becoming overwhelming for Isaac on this dark winter night. Isaac told Becky he'd call her back, returning to Ana who was gone.

Before Isaac could call either of them back, Ana called back and berated Isaac for disconnecting her, which, technically, he hadn't. Then Mrs. Hyde dropped a bombshell, so to speak.

"Isaac, our daughter is in trouble," she simply said.

Isaac pepped up and felt his heart race, though he purposely remained calm for Ana's sake.

"Exactly what kind?" he asked maturely.

"She has way too much free time, and is hanging out with what I'd call the 'wrong crowd,'" Ana explained. "I'm tired when I get off work, it's late, and she's not always there, though she does return."

Isaac kept listening intently, thinking of a response, wondering why there wasn't a "framework" of rules to live by. Wouldn't that make it all so simpler.

"As far as I know, she's not sneaking out, since no one she knows drives, and I peek into her room late at night, but she's also becoming impious. And she seems mad at me and also you, for not being around," Ana confessed. "I'm going nuts here, Isaac."

Isaac loved when Ana used big words like "impious" to describe a person. But truly, he gulped, knowing the past few months had built up to this point, which he half anticipated. Should he offer to come home, ask to talk more about this situation in the morning, or in a few days? Was Ana being an alarmist or overly negative? Should he give in to her, knowing she was in an emotional state? Or was Ana substituting Lauren for something going on with herself?

Isaac changed the subject away from Lauren, and back to Ana, her heath and finances. He felt this was the most prudent way to handle the ordeal.

Ana would have none of this, and asked Isaac if he wanted to discuss Lauren's behavior "in more detail" tomorrow night. Isaac, knowing this was his way out, at least for 24 hours, agreed. They hung up. Isaac called Becky for advice and "to talk" as he remembered Becky had phoned him while he was dealing with life back on the home front.

Isaac was mentally exhausted from his conversation with Ana as well as adjusting to being back in Knoxville in what he deemed the "doldrums" of the year. Though it was warmer than New Jersey, it was still dark, gloomy and chilly, and while the basketball teams were in action on various weeknights, the campus seemed dead without football on the weekends. Instead of chatting with Becky that evening, Isaac suggested they meet up at his place tomorrow night. Becky was busy with her pregnancy, Travis, and much else, so she suggested coming Sunday night to Isaac's place.

When Becky arrived, she looked and seemed different that when Isaac last saw her prior to the holidays; it was not long before Isaac understood why. While things were sliding downhill in his life, the same was true for Becky, as she and Travis were on rocky terms due to issues surrounding their future child.

The issue at hand was the future of Becky's pregnancy and Travis' paternal role, or perhaps lack thereof. Despite his military service and current career, Becky said Travis could be immature. She sensed he was scared of his impending fatherhood. Due to this, Travis was now urging Becky to at least consider an abortion. Becky was 100% against this murderous idea, and thus an impasse had come about. Like a veteran relief pitcher, Isaac Hyde was summoned. He had his own issues, but was willing to give advice as best he could.

Isaac and Becky talked for nearly two hours, but made little progress. Isaac was no psychologist but tried to assuage Becky as best he could, telling her he empathized with her, and basically "sided" with her, so she'd feel better and eventually leave him to recuperate and ponder his own goings-on. But Becky was a strange girl, very self-deprecating and started blaming herself. Nothing Isaac said was going to change her feelings that perhaps Travis was correct and that she'd made mistakes and was "a bad person."

Most northern girls Isaac had dated rarely talked in such harsh and brutally honest terms about themselves, no matter the situation. Eventually Isaac simply froze and suggested Becky go get some sleep and try to take her mind off the ordeal. That was easier said than done, and Becky was discouraged, telling Isaac she now understood he "wanted nothing to do with her."

Even at this point, that was far from the truth. But before Isaac could explain, she was headed for his apartment door. Isaac tried to stop her and grabbed her; she pushed him away. Isaac did not know what to do, so he did the right thing, and let her go. Then he pondered whether she was in driving condition and moved toward the car to assist. Becky collapsed. "Oh shit" Isaac thought, thinking about this scene outside, with her and the baby. It was like a movie, and a bad one, in the Appalachian hills. He actually chuckled for a second.

Isaac went to help Becky up and she arose, falling into his arms with tears streaming. Isaac walked her back into the house and made some hot tea. The unborn baby seemed fine, or so Becky said.

The two decided to cease talking about the situation, especially Becky, who was somewhat embarrassed. By the time they were done drinking tea and talking about various matters, the sun was rising and both, realizing they did not have morning classes, tried to get some sleep. Isaac offered Becky his bed over and over, but she said the couch would be fine. Finally, Isaac relented and went to his bedroom. Four hours later, around 10am, Isaac awoke with a woman next to his side for the first time in weeks.

Of course, it was Becky, not Ana, and since there was nothing nefarious involved, he felt happy to be able to comfort someone in need. Isaac assumed Becky felt the same. As she awoke, Becky looked pleasant, opened one eye to see him, then smiled and closed her eye. Ten seconds later, she opened both eyes violently and jumped up. Isaac was taken aback.

"What happened?" Becky yelled at him.

"Um, nothing. We talked." Isaac quickly replied with a smile and a confused look.

"Are you sure?" Becky asked, a look of fear in her eyes now.

"Sure, about what?" said Isaac.

"That nothing happened!" Becky said with a glare.

"What would have happened? You slept. Becky, I am old enough to be your father," he added, again with a smile. "You were upset about Travis and we talked."

Becky was clearly becoming delusional. Then before Isaac could finish the rest of his sentence, Becky grabbed a few personal items and said, "Well, this is too weird. I think we need time apart. I hope you're not lying."

At this point, Isaac mused again about "the scene" that was transpiring for people in the neighborhood to view. Isaac suddenly felt uncomfortable, and shocked at Becky's accusations and attitude. Then again, how well did he know this girl? He thought about her upbringing, and what Travis might think, even though "nothing happened."

Where Isaac was raised, and when he was in college, this situation would arise and it was understandable. He now wondered if it was the same in 2009 in eastern Tennessee. He was actually a bit worried.

As Becky left, looking disheveled, he again reiterated to her that he was trying to help and Becky just looked back with a sardonic nod.

And that was that.

Isaac could not believe that he, a married man of 45, would have to be given the third degree by this 20-something, when nothing malevolent had occurred.

Mr. Hyde's "mid-winter of frustrations" had just gotten worse.

13

With Ana distant, and after the Becky/Travis ordeal, Isaac had to get away. Presidents Day presented a three day weekend, and even though school was technically in session, Isaac's sentient professor had cancelled class in honor of our esteemed leaders. Why universities were closed for Martin Luther King Day yet operated on Presidents Day, Columbus Day and Veterans Day was another ugly subject Isaac had mused and written about, but for now, he couldn't be bothered with those issues.

The Smokies seemed too close, so he chose the state capital in Nashville, a few hours to the west on Interstate 40.

Nashville, Tennessee, is a historic, fantastic city. Few would disagree with that assessment of "NashVegas." It may not be the quietest place to "clear his head" as Isaac's plan was, but it seemed to make sense at this juncture on another cold weekend in the doldrums of late February in Middle Tennessee. Isaac wanted to not only think about Ana's bickering, but Becky, and life and death as well.

Isaac had been to Nashville close to half a dozen times, but again, either as a child or with family; he had never gone on his own as an adult or with friends his age. For a change, Isaac was ready to blow off some steam.

During the two-hour trek west on I-40 about a week after the Ana/Becky/Travis debacle, Isaac phoned Ana. He had yet to speak to Becky in the days since, and surely was not planning on bringing that topic up with Ana; the Hydes had more important matters.

"How are you, honey?" Isaac quickly asked, looking to take control of the conversation and mollify any of Ana's haranguing.

"Good," was Ana's short reply.

"How's Lauren?" was his next question.

"Better, slightly better," Ana noted.

Ana was rarely laconic, but this was fine with Isaac as he prepared to launch into his explanation of his overnight "Nashville Run."

After Isaac explained that he needed to clear his head, Ana was surprisingly understanding, if not somewhat jealous or condescending. Isaac could not tell which, though.

Since their last few conversations had been similar – not necessarily amicable, but rather short and tame – Isaac moved to end the talk, saying he'd check in tomorrow evening, when Ana dropped another bombshell.

"Isaac, Lauren's sneaked out two nights ago," she stated monotonously.

Isaac was dumbfounded, not knowing if he needed to pull over to the side of the desolate highway to devote full attention, or just keep listening.

"And…" he stammered.

"And what? I found her stripping on the corner for drunk men at $5 a pop," Ana said sarcastically.

"Well, where did she go? How long did it take you to realize she was gone?" Isaac asked confidently, again in an attempt to turn the situation into one he could control, since Ana was responsible.

Ana explained that Lauren had simply gone to some party with girls and a few guys, where, as far as Ana could tell once she got wind of the info from another mom, there was no alcohol or drugs. Parents were nearby, and the only "inappropriate behavior" involved the kids sitting in the family's Jacuzzi.

Isaac felt relieved, sort of.

Ana then told Isaac she had grounded Lauren for a week with no phone, TV or computer. Isaac thought that a bit harsh, but decided not to share that opinion. He couldn't afford to, he felt.

Ana said she relented on the computer solely for internet usage via homework and said Lauren was allowed TV after two days. Isaac felt better.

"She took it hard, began crying, saying she hated me and you, and so on," Ana said.

Isaac felt his heart break and indeed felt helpless and remained silent on the phone. Not knowing what else to say, he searched his mind for a non-sequitur, but found none.

They chatted for a few more minutes, and hung up with some pleasantries, almost feeling as though the situation was resolved and Lauren would learn her lesson.

Isaac then asked, half-jokingly, "Did she really say she hated me too? I wasn't even there."

Ana guffawed and explained that she was clearly rebelling against both of them, for different reasons. Ana did share that Lauren said she "wanted to go live with dad in Tennessee."

They both laughed at that, feeling glad Lauren did not have a drivers' license or much money of her own.

"Isaac, do you think we'll make it?" Ana asked softly.

It was a line Ana often used when they were engaged, then again when their marriage was in its infancy. She hadn't said it in at least a decade though.

"Baby...," Isaac said back, with a kind tone.

"I'm serious," Ana confirmed.

"Do you mean with the kids, our lives, financially, or with these next few months until I return?" he asked.

"The latter," Ana replied quickly.

"Sure, sweetheart. Just think positively. We've made it through worse, I think," he said.

"I hope so," Ana affirmed. "And honey, if we use our heads while also following our hearts, and with a little help from our faith, we have a chance."

Impressed, and wondering if Ana made that up or got it from somewhere, Isaac chose to capitalize on that upbeat note, even if quixotic.

"Could not have said or explained it better myself, dear," he stated calmly.

Ana agreed and said good-bye, wishing him safe travels.

Isaac proceeded to Nashville.

Upon arrival, one such as Isaac realizes the difference between the 'Villes -- Nash and Knox – rather quickly: Nashville is much bigger, more modern, perhaps less "personal," yet quieter, at least in the daytime. Indeed, Nashville is the second largest metropolitan area in the state after Memphis, but just seemed so large to Isaac after his months in Knoxville and because he had not see any major city other than New York in close to a year. Also, though Nashville has numerous colleges, most are private and outside downtown, unlike UT, which dominates much of Knoxville and serves as the city's number one employer.

Like most metropolises, Nashville seemed much less crowded, cleaner, cheaper and friendlier than Manhattan. It also was pretty. Hills, though not quite green yet, dotted his drive in, from the north, south and even west. Basically all directions piqued Isaac's historical and geographical interest as he recalled some Civil War history as well as other Nashville tales from the past:

Andrew Jackson had once practiced law here after relocating from the neighboring state of North Carolina, which had once owned all the land that became Tennessee. He left to go fight in the closing battles of the War of 1812, some 15 years prior to his being elected our 7th president. Nashville was already a city, having been chartered in 1806, a decade after Tennessee was admitted to the union as our 16th state. Jackson was one of the state's first US senators in 1797. Of course, by 1826 Nashville was the state's capital.

Like Atlanta, Charleston, Chattanooga, Savannah and Richmond, Nashville was a much desired city during the American Civil War. And though much like Atlanta, many of its battlefields have been overrun by suburbs and urban sprawl, there is still much to learn and see.

Nashville had "hosted" civil war battles in the 1860s, with a few in, or on the immediate outskirts of the city, in places like Franklin to the immediate south. As the capital of one of the key confederate states, second only to Virginia, Nashville was much desired by Federal forces, especially due to its prime real estate as a shipping port on the vast Cumberland River. Nashville was, in fact the first southern state capital to fall into union occupation early in 1862 after the north seized Fort Donelson, in Stewart County, 80 or so miles to the northwest of Nashville.

Again in 1864, Nashville was at the center of the storm, during the so-called Franklin-Nashville campaign. This took place during the fall and the closing days of the War for the Union, as General Sherman concurrently marched southeast through Atlanta "to the sea" for five weeks to give President Lincoln Savannah and the south as a Christmas present on December 22.

After a one-day Federal win at nearby Franklin, Nashville was fortified on the south by the Confederates, but it was no use; the city was taken two weeks later during a two-day battle within the city limits on

December 15 and 16. Over six thousand confederate soldiers died in both Franklin and Nashville. Warfare in the Western Theatre essentially ended after these union victories.

These thoughts soon ended in Isaac's mind as he propelled toward downtown on a sunny, but chilly, Sunday afternoon.

Isaac first sought out a nice, downtown hotel for a brief stay. Money, for once, was to be no object for 24 hours or so. He had fewer expenses these days, and also allowed himself this freedom since he had not been away much, locally. Mr. Hyde stepped up and chose the Hermitage Hotel, right above downtown, next to the state capitol complex. The building was a century old, quite pricy, but worth it right now in Isaac's life.

He entered the ornate lobby and handed his reservation to charming-looking southern lady dressed in yellow, whose nametag said "Natalie." After being assigned a 7th level room, Isaac attempted to glean more of the building's history from her. She was up to the task.

"Well, Mr. Hyde," she began in a confident voice, "the hotel was named after President Andrew Jackson's nearby estate, and, at the time, was "'Nashville's first million dollar hotel.'" Isaac wished he had a tape recorder or pen for this information.

"The Hermitage basically became gathering place for the city's aristocrats and visiting celebrities as well as war heroes, she said. "Even presidents such like Taft, Wilson, Roosevelt, Johnson and Nixon visited."

Isaac leaned in, explaining he was a historian "on assignment" and asked for more information on the 19th or early 20th century. Natalie knew no more, but she did boast, as though quoting from a brochure, that "The Hermitage essentially announced Nashville's arrival on the scene as a major southern city." Isaac politely smiled, thanked her and headed for his room, where he learned via internet that during its beginnings, the hotel was utilized as a "platform" for pro and anti suffrage forces; radio programs and orchestras also took place between its walls.

Isaac truly loved this hotel, not only for all the historic reasons, but for its comfort level, which he was unused to from all his "roughing it" when traveling over the years, especially in his youth. He took a two hour nap, grabbed a shower, put on a new shirt he got for Christmas and went out to see the sights.

Cold as it was, Nashville was hopping, being that this area honored Presidents Day and thus, most people were off Monday.

Nashville defined diversity when ambling through its historic streets. Not just the buildings, but the people. They were a mix of young and old, tourist and local, but also black and white – in reality "urban," not "southern," blacks and country music loving whites. And though there were clubs and other establishments clearly designed for each sect, many intermeshed, for better or worse. Southern stereotypes had been quickly dismissed.

Isaac peered into many of the restaurants and clubs, deciding against patronizing many of them settling on a classy place called "Demo's," which, though crowded, was a fine choice. He dined on steak and spaghetti for a very good price. Then Isaac moved back into the city for a nightcap.

Forty-five minutes later, Isaac was polishing off his second and last beer while yucking it up with a couple slightly younger than he. They talked sports, politics, culture and so on. The guy and gal, originally from southeastern Kentucky, now lived just south of Nashville, in the hills between Pulaski and Murfreesboro. The latter being the sights of the famous Battle of Stones River, while former was most notorious for being the birthplace of the Ku Klux Klan, formed by southern Democrats after the Civil War. These two well-dressed, educated folks knew and cared more about history than most people Isaac knew, including some of his co-workers. They had much in common with Isaac as they picked his mind about the north, while he inquired about their rural background and current status.

"The South is an interesting place to study, as I'm sure you know, because it still retains a lot of its historical identity where other areas of the United States have since lost that," David said at one point.

"I don't really know why that is; maybe it's because of heavy immigration into other areas or something, but it generally seems to be true – though Atlanta and Charlotte could be considered exceptions nowadays," Kristi later added with a smile as she ordered another apple martini.

Dave and Kristi had met at Belmont University in Nashville, a small, local private college. They married a year after graduation, and though just in their mid 30s, had three kids, all school age, their oldest in 6th grade already. With their life experiences, they were clearly mature and Isaac enjoyed the chat, since he had only been with college kids lately, aside from his wife and their "do gooder" northeastern friends. David and Kristi were weekly churchgoers, deep thinkers and charming.

Isaac did not want to explain his entire reason for being in Tennessee, but he did want to share his unique views on the south based upon his residence and travels. "Look, guys, I've tried to do a lot to dispel ignorant notions about your part of America," he smirked while grabbing David's' arm. "I haven't convinced any of my family and friends to move out of this way yet, but maybe they have a better understanding after hearing some stories from me rather than Hollywood."

"You haven't seen any white sheets or burning crosses, have you?" David then said, with a huge guffaw. Folks eavesdropping around the group burst into laughter. "Nah, the uneducated folks are kind, and most of the wealthy types aren't disingenuous like a John Edwards or an Al Gore." Isaac let out a huge belly laugh.

As Isaac was seeking a departure, not worried about being slightly inebriated since he was walking, Kristi, apparently oblivious to his wedding ring, asked Isaac if she could call over their friend, Monica, so he could meet her. Isaac pointed to his ring, but Kristi ignored him. As Monica sat down, Isaac noticed she was stunning. In fact, she looked very much like Ana, just 10-15 years younger. Isaac's heart belonged to his wife, now and forever. He quickly made his marriage and life obvious before they chatted further. As the conversation unwound, Monica had a few adult beverages and perhaps forgot Isaac was happily married and continuously pulled his hand to dance, something Isaac told her he doesn't do with his own wife, much less a strange woman. The night ended harmlessly with Isaac sauntering back to his prestigious hotel, happy that he had a pleasant night and feeling young at heart, if nothing else.

"King" Isaac awoke Monday morning to bountiful sunshine and a pleasant 50 degree late winter day in Middle Tennessee. He was to make this day about sight-seeing and history. The world, or at least Nashville, was his opus. And he intended to digest it fully.

After a jaunt down the college area near Vanderbilt and some scouting out of the local blues clubs outside downtown – all closed until the evening – he wound up parking along the Cumberland River, with a great view of the Tennessee Titans football stadium. This river had an interesting history, much from the Civil War. The Cumberland connected many of the great towns and battlefields of Northern Tennessee and surrounding states. In fact, it moves nearly 700 miles from the Appalachian mountains of extreme southeastern Kentucky to its western "mouth" at the Ohio River near the southern tip of Illinois.

Isaac paused for many minutes to watch steamboats and barges move along the river's snaky trek each way. Many undoubtedly moved toward the various dams, recreation areas, lakes and reservoirs created by the Army Corps of Engineers in the 1930s and again in the 1980s. He was at the edge of downtown, about 100 feet above the water, standing atop a levee erected as a bulwark for protection from any storms. A riverwalk that hosted several local War Memorials to Tennessee's brave veterans from the War of 1812 through today's Global War on Terror was also adjacent. It was a picturesque, all-American sight to see in one of the hearts of the South.

A nod to the country-western district later, Isaac hiked up "Printers Alley," back past his hotel and to the state capitol building. The capital area, from the highway and street, looked rather bland and austere, especially with the capitol's dome not actually being a dome but rather a point. However, once he entered the gated-off area, Isaac was somewhat impressed. War Memorials dotted the brick and marble covered landscape, with the World War One Memorial displaying some great architecture, framing some of the federal buildings. It was much like Richmond or Montgomery, which certainly made sense. The view from atop the stairs leading up to the state capitol was exquisite on all sides, with a mix of brown and green at every angle. A statue of Andrew Jackson, one of the few Democrats Isaac admired in terms of military attributes, sat atop a horse in warrior-like fashion, as well he should.

A figurative tip of the cap to the history G-ds, another walk through the plaza, a stroll through more of the touristy streets and a drive around the city's perimeter later and Isaac was pressing east, away from a slightly dipping sun, toward his "home" in Knoxville. He had his "peace" and was in a better mood.

14

"Lauren is missing."

Those were not exactly the three words Isaac longed to here on his voice mail when he finally checked, somewhere east of Nashville, near the city of Cookeville.

Ana was, unfortunately, quite serious and furious that she'd been unable to reach her husband for the past few hours. When he honestly told he left the phone in the car, which was a rare occurrence, she was not placated.

"Isaac, she was not here when I came to her room this morning around 10 to see if she was up," Ana stammered.

Isaac kept listening.

"And no one has heard from her," Ana said. "None of her friends, their parents, Ross, the neighbors…"

Isaac kept listening, driving faster, and began to feel his heart race, pondering what could have gone awry, why and how.

"Isaac honey, what do you think happened? Am I to blame?," Ana asked.

Isaac thought long and hard about how to approach this tenuous situation as he refused to sound insouciant.

"Ana, first of all, you are NOT to blame. Teenagers do stupid things," he said with confidence. "As for what to do now, give me five minutes and I'll call you right back."

To Isaac's pleasure, Ana agreed, without an argument.

Unfortunately to Isaac's chagrin, he had no idea what to say or do, but he did need time to think. He called the only people who might know how to approach this matter: his parents in Arizona.

David Hyde answered, and his son briefly elaborated upon the recent "issues" surrounding Lauren's demeanor and ordeals with behavior, as his father listened intently. When Isaac was done rambling, David took a deep breath and said very succinctly:

"Isaac, call back and ask her if she tried Lauren's cell phone."

Isaac laughed, informing his dad that he was certain Ana did that first.

"Are you sure, Isaac?" David asked, in a serious tone.

"Well, I didn't ask her, but I didn't think I needed to," he explained. "Ana's not dumb."

David urged Isaac to "immediately call her back and ask that specific question."

Isaac did. Ana had not. They laughed nervously, and Ana tried the cell phone. She called Isaac back a minute later saying the phone went directly to voice mail. Isaac phoned his dad back to explain.

David was just about to give Isaac his next suggestion, when Ana called his other line. She said Lauren just called her back. Isaac quickly switched over to his dad, told him he'd keep him posted, then went back to Ana.

"She said she's okay and not to worry," Ana stated matter-of-factly.

"And…?" Isaac said timorously.

"Oh, and that she'd call me in a few hours, after she did some thinking."

Isaac was dumbfounded but comforted by Ana's relaxed nature. But he was scrupulous by nature and needed details, at least a location?

Ana told him that Lauren said she was safe, "not far from town" and would hopefully "be back soon."

Isaac, realizing it was fruitless to attempt to get more information from his obstinate wife in this situation, said, "Okay, I guess. Keep me posted. Love you." And he hung up.

And waited.

And drove as fast he could through the hills and turns toward Knoxville on Interstate 40. He refused even to detour in the vast and picturesque mountains of Cumberland County, where some of Tennessee's highest peaks, like Walden Ridge's Hinch Mountain, at over 3,000 feet sat. Nor did Isaac seek out the rugged paths toward lovely Chattanooga or northeastern Alabama's Guntersville Lake where the Civil War's vital Tullahoma Campaign occurred. To Isaac, a historian who might never be in these areas again, this meant Lauren was a priority.

Why Isaac was hurrying was unapparent to him, as he could do as little to ameliorate the situation in his Knoxville apartment as he could from his car, but nonetheless, he moved with great alacrity.

Upon his arrival, Isaac got quite the surprise. Two young ladies sat on the steps near his apartment. He recognized both.

"Hi, daddy!" Lauren said, as if she was greeting him upon his arrival back from a work day, and that nothing was abnormal about this situation.

"Hey, Isaac," Becky said, also nonchalantly, with a smile.

Isaac was infuriated at both, for different reasons, of course.

"I always wanted a big sister," said Lauren, truly trying to avoid the situation and questions for as long as possible.

Where to begin, Isaac mulled. He felt like he was on the brink of a nervous breakdown. First, and least importantly, he was pleased to see Becky seemed uninterested in holding an unhealthy grudge from their quarrel a few nights back. As for Lauren, she was in Knoxville, had found his home, and Ana knew none of this. In some way, Isaac was impressed with how Lauren accomplished this, but also very curious and, as he felt a father should be, was perplexed and angry.

"Let's go inside, girls," he said in as grave a tone as he could muster, gesticulating with his right hand in the manner of an orchestra conductor.

Lauren stood by Isaac's small couch near his window, observing her father's temporary home, smiling in that condescending way that teenage girls do. Isaac was not amused, figuring the last thing his little daughter should be doing is conveying a cavalier attitude about this situation, even though she had arrived safely.

Isaac offered both girls a soda, then sat down, much like a coach or school principal would do to "manage" a difficult situation. He sensed both girls were flustered, especially Lauren, and just trying to give the auspice of calmness so that he would not become enraged.

Isaac knew this would not work with the two new "friends" together.

"Becky, I'm not nearly as peeved at you as this one," Isaac said, gesturing toward his daughter. "In fact, you and I can easily get through whatever it is we're dealing with, so I'll talk to you later. Will you excuse me and my daughter?"

Pregnant Becky popped up, said good bye to Lauren, and departed. Isaac hoped she'd be okay.

Through an abrasive but honest talk, Isaac determined that Lauren had an older friend pick her up last night, let her stay at her house, then dropped her at the local train station this morning. From that point, Lauren took the train to Manhattan's Penn Station, somehow found a route toward Knoxville paid and boarded. This was all discussed via conference call with Ana back home, who was understandably furious with her daughter, but avoided becoming irascible.

Lauren had at least wisely taken a route that had no major transfers or overnight layovers, and thus, arrived in Knoxville at a reasonable hour, then took a shuttle to the university area. She had her dad's address handy and walked over, where Becky was just arriving. Of course, not only had the two girls never met, but they'd never heard of each other.

Isaac was reticent to change the subject, but did temporarily let Lauren off the hook by inquiring as to what she and Becky spoke about.

"Why, dad?" she answered shrewdly.

"Because Becky and I are friends; that's why," Isaac quipped back.

"She's a bit young," Lauren said with a snicker.

"She…is…a…friend," Isaac said patronizingly, looking down at Lauren with a fatherly smirk. "And a classmate," he added brusquely.

Isaac's explication was simple and unnecessary. Lauren understood the whole time, and was just trying to distract him from the crux of the matter.

Lauren explained that she had only arrived at Isaac's place a few minutes before he returned. It was a plausible story. She had briefly told Becky who she in fact was and why she was in Knoxville, then asked the same of Becky. Becky noted she was "a close friend who was coming to apologize to Isaac" and Lauren relayed that this was "about where the discussion ended."

Isaac, assuming Lauren was not being specious, was pleased and decided to drop this topic and move toward an end to the discussion of Lauren's surprise "road trip," at least for this evening. It was late, and both Hydes, for similar reasons, were clearly exhausted

15

After something of a restless night for Isaac on his couch, since Lauren commandeered the bed, the phone rang far too early the next morning.

"Dad, mom's on the phone," Lauren screamed, forgetting Isaac was about six feet away from her, not at the other end of their 2,000 square foot New Jersey home.

In a fog, Isaac was confused for a moment at the sound of his daughter's voice, then recalled the prior night's "festivities."

He was still partly in the opaque state, when he rubbed his eyes and looked up to see a woman handing him the phone. But that "woman" was his daughter.

Isaac had seen his "little girl" just over a month ago, but with all the rush and commotion of the holidays, he didn't spend as much time with her as he wished. He had not really enjoyed her company in nearly six months. Lauren was 15 next week, and she looked it. Isaac had met Ana when Ana was not yet 23, so Lauren was fewer than eight years younger than that right now. Couple this with Lauren's very professional clothing she still had on from last evening and her mature behavior in "organizing a road trip" down to see dad in Tennessee, and Lauren Hyde no longer seemed such a child. This was clear as she began to attempt to cook some sort of breakfast from whatever remained in Isaac's fridge and pantry.

"Isaac!" Ana yelled into the phone, arousing Isaac from his reflection.

"What's wrong?" Ana brayed.

"Nothing," he answered. "In fact, our mature daughter is cooking her dad some breakfast."

"Mature?" Ana yelled. "Do you remember why she is there, sir?"

Isaac paused, pondering how to answer this question, as he knew the "wrong" answer could swing this conversation very badly. Isaac whispered to Lauren half-jokingly, "Why *are* you here?" Lauren laughed and told him it was to get away from mom and bond with dad, and to check out prospective colleges. She moved rapidly back and forth from kitchen to living room like an unattended lawnmower.

Before Isaac could give the all-important response, Ana piped in:

"Have you talked with her, and explained to her the dangers of what she did, at her age…"

Isaac knew not to joke around and try to keep this simple until the three of them could talk or until more time had elapsed.

"Yes, we're dealing with it…slowly," he answered, smiling, and telling Lauren he wanted three eggs.

"Ok, well, I'm at work now, so please assure me you're taking care of it and that our daughter will be on her way home soon," Ana pleaded.

Isaac decided not to answer the second part of the question, since it was not like Lauren was at some friend's house or unknown village with strangers.

"Yes, we'll talk. I'll call you later," he answered calmly.

Ana, always assiduous, needed to get back to work, so she relented with an "OK, thanks."

Lauren then brought out some bagels, eggs and ersatz coffee from a seldom-used can she located in the pantry. Isaac and his daughter then began a private breakfast in the hills of eastern Tennessee. It was incumbent upon them eat and chat, as father and daughter had some catching up to do.

Isaac began by complimenting Lauren on her professional display in procuring transportation to Knoxville, though he did query as to how an underage girl was able to do all of this. Lauren explained she used her friend's mom's credit card and was going to pay her back. No one at any train station seemed to ask her for anything other than a photo identification to pick up the tickets, for which she used her school ID card. Again, no one noticed the school's name or lack of proof of birth date? With her current outfit of formal jacket, sweater vest, collared shirt and slacks, she could have passed for a 19 year-old intern at some Manhattan office. Surely the engineers of the train noticed nothing abnormal in this brown-eyed girl. After all, many folks over 16 or 17 still did not have drivers' licenses, due to New York City's massive public transportation outfit.

Isaac decided not to further lecture, nor compliment, but rather to find out what effectuated her plan? *Why* Lauren had decided to become mutinous and run away from home? It sounded so awful, like something from a *Lifetime* movie, but this was reality, and dad needed answers, seeking to put his mind somewhat at ease.

Lauren was mad at her mother, not so much her father. This was expected, especially with Isaac not being in town. She wanted to go to parties, hang out with guys, have a later curfew, ---all normal requests of a 9th grader. Ana would not budge. Ana was conservative through and through, and wanted her daughter to grow up as productive, safe and healthy as she did. Overall, Isaac agreed. There was nothing he'd complain about with Ana in that department, so he backed her. That said, the Hydes were not overprotective, or else they'd never let Lauren go to some of the functions she did or wear the outfits she occasionally donned in the summer.

Isaac, like Ana the psychologist would do with a client, listened intently as his daughter, tears flowing at times, poured her little heart out about the past year or two, but mostly the six months since Isaac left, since she was now in high school with new pressures and ambitions. For a moment, as they were not in their home, Isaac almost sensed Lauren looked at him as a psychologist or at the very least a friend. In this instance, it was cathartic, thus acceptable.

Like her dad and mom, Lauren did few things pell-mell. She explained she'd been pondering the surreptitious escape down to dad's since the tumultuous morning after he left in early January. She saved some money, thought of the safety factor, logistics and consequence for her actions, which she figured might be severe. Deep, deep inside, Isaac was impressed, even proud, but knew Ana was not, so he never relayed that "confession" to his daughter.

"Dad, I just don't know anymore," she confessed, while picking at her waffles and cereal.

"Don't know what?" Isaac asked, truly perplexed.

"About anything, what I want to do in life, who I'm mad at or why…" Lauren answered.

"Um, sweetheart, you just started high school; you have time to worry."

Lauren explained that wasn't exactly what she meant, but in her mind, she really did not know how to explain her thoughts, since they were so jumbled. She wished she kept a diary. Written form was always easier for Lauren to relay than oral form.

But Lauren was priggish, and therefore her mindset made her feel the need to properly explain her fears and concerns to her dad. Secretly, she wished her mom was there, as Ana would or might understand. Lauren just hadn't felt like sitting down with her mom too often lately. Even though Lauren was a teenager and acting up, because she was 14, Ross, at 10, seemed to garner most of Ana's attention when it came to "missing dad" and matters like that.

Hence, the clandestine romp to the southwest was perhaps Lauren's way of rebelling and getting her some attention. And she explained that to her dad, even using the word "clandestine" to impress him, since it had been a vocabulary word in school the week prior.

Dad and Lauren went round and round for another hour or so, until an understanding was reached. Isaac, not really in charge of Lauren's daily life right now, explained to his daughter that she was "halfway through the battle" and now needed to "present that same case" to her mom, which would be tougher.

"Above all else, just be as honest with her as you were with me," he advised. "The truth may not set you free, but may reduce your sentence or punishment, and plus you'll feel better." Lauren smiled. It made Isaac melt, just the same as it did when she was three year old toddler.

The two of them called Ana and arranged for Lauren to fly home the next afternoon, thus limiting Lauren's missed days of school and enabling Isaac to get back to his daily duties, which had been interrupted by Lauren's visit, Becky's issues and Isaac's own sudden guilt which was now telling him to consider eschewing the final nine or so weeks of class and head home.

It was now nearly dark out, and Isaac told Ana he'd take Lauren to dinner tonight, she'd stay over again, then they'd spend some more time together the following day, before he'd bring her to Knoxville's McGhee-Tyson airport where she'd fly to DC then to JFK. The ticket was close to $500, since it was booked only 24 hours prior to departure. That was nearly five times what it would take in gas to drive back, but this was easier. Lauren's train ticket was $125 one way. She was a smart buyer to boot.

16

The following morning, after a nice dinner and ice cream in downtown Knoxville the prior evening, Isaac and Lauren both slept in. But by the time Isaac arose, he realized he had just a few short, precious hours left with his daughter until May. He also was wrestling with returning home and still had a small, covert desire to just head back north with his daughter, and either scratch the rest of the semester for good or temporarily. Isaac was already frustrated with his alternate life and now knew family was more important than anything. His professors understanding his predicament, were equitable, and thus gave Isaac some "ultimatums" when he informed them of his issues.

Isaac wanted advice. But at this stage, where could *he* turn at a time when everyone wanted *his* advice?

As far as he knew, Becky still somewhat mad at him. Isaac had not heard from her since Lauren arrived, and prior to that, they weren't speaking. Therefore, he obviated her from consideration. Ana was busy, and Isaac also was unsure if he wanted to tell his wife these new ideas. Lauren was a kid, who'd likely have an emotional response, such as "yes, daddy, come home! Come home now!"

Not that she was totally wrong, but on the other hand, couldn't Isaac "tough" out three more months, especially as the weather would be turning, and he was well over half done with this odyssey? Isaac thought so, and knew Ana would too. Since he'd spent so much time away already, she'd demand he finished what he started.

Nonetheless, Lauren's unexpected visit turned out to be the best times Isaac had had in months, for he and his only daughter had rarely spent private time together when at home since she was little. They walked first through campus, stopping to admire architecture and the views from the hilltop quads.

The intransigence that had engulfed Lauren's 14 year-old personality the past few years was gone while she was "on vacation" with her dad in a new place, and it was a glorious 55 degree sunny day to boot!

After a walk along the river, through downtown Knoxville, both campus and actual downtown, and a stoic trek through the historic churches and city buildings, the Hydes enjoyed a pleasurable Italian meal at an establishment Isaac had plucked out prior to the holidays at the recommendation of Becky.

Which made Isaac think of Becky. Though he wanted to devote his entire attention to Lauren until she departed, he needed to reconcile with his friend. He needed to speak to her and, whether he wanted to or not, apologize. This was the kind of person his parents raised. Isaac also wanted to "confront" Travis, although not in an emotional or angry way. He felt the need not only to implore Travis not to force or coerce Becky into terminating her pregnancy out of "convenience," but also to clarify what he thought Travis just might suspect: that Becky and Isaac were becoming too close. This was, of course, verifiably false. If anything, Becky looked to Isaac as a father figure, nothing more. Travis should realize that, but Isaac wanted to be sure.

Isaac sought all this "resolution" just in case he decided to follow Lauren in the coming days and permanently return to the Garden State. And even if not, Isaac Hyde was the type who loathed tension in his life and brooding amongst his acquaintances. So even if Travis and Becky were of the opposite mindset, Isaac would step up and do the right thing – in many ways.

Isaac was in a jovial mood as he and Lauren arrived at the airport. Lauren, expectedly, was the polar opposite. And though she did not know that part of the reason Isaac was peppy was due to his potential decision to return home, Isaac tried to act as though Lauren was being unnecessarily lugubrious. She instead became more perplexed.

"Dad, I don't want to go home," she muttered, very unconvincingly. It was so cliché that Isaac didn't really think she was upset, but just wanted to say it for effect.

"Honey, just a few more months," he explained to his daughter. "When spring comes and the weather warms, daddy will be home right behind it."

Isaac sounded like he was talking to a six year old, not a girl closing in on her 15th birthday. But, it seemed as though Lauren wanted to be babied now.

"I know, I know, dad," she confessed, with a smile. "I just enjoyed our time together, even though it was short. And I don't look forward to going back to school…and the wrath of mom!"

They both laughed, and Isaac sent Lauren on her way, then motored back through the barren hills to downtown Knoxville to contact Becky and make some decisions on the upcoming three months.

17

So Isaac had some issues and decisions, beginning with Becky and Travis. These two folks weren't of relation, nor pertinent to anything in his future after May, but as a mature man in his 40s, he felt he should speak to them and ideally aid them positively.

Becky and Travis, though often recalcitrant, and in Travis's case, leery, were thankfully open to meeting with Isaac, in what he felt was something of an "exit meeting." Isaac wanted to let Travis know he was innocuous, but also to try, one last time, to give the young couple some well thought out advice. They met at Travis's condo, on the outskirts of town.

Upon entering, Isaac knew why Becky liked Travis, for better or worse. Despite his blue collar upbringing and her middle class, educated background, they had very similar taste. This was evident from the artwork on the walls, perhaps purchased by Becky, kitchenware and even the carpet, which was hardly "manly." Though the two had dated for nearly four years and were expecting a child together, they lived separately. This gave Becky time for her studies and Travis space for himself, but moreover, they were serious, religious folks; their parents and they all agreed that living together came after marriage, or baby, perhaps. Books and studies, along with personal anecdotes from the failed marriages of their impulsive friends, had shown them that marriages survive longer when co-habitation begins after the vows are exchanged. It seemed, overall, to work. Isaac and Ana had done the same.

Isaac came in and sat down and began to enjoy some sweet tea Becky made.

"Guys, this does not have to be so formal," Isaac explained. "But since I care about y'all, and since I'm not sure if I'll be hanging around as much in the next few months, I wanted you to have time to yourself, but also talk to you once more."

Isaac had told Ana about what he'd say to them, and Ana had offered her opinion. Most of it focused around "celebrating life" as Ana deemed it, ensuring that Travis and Becky would not have an abortion, keep their baby, or at the very least, offer it for adoption and try again, once married.

As noted, Isaac had grown up in the "typical Jewish" family where people were pro-choice. It's not that they didn't find abortion an awful process for women and certainly nascent child, but they had been taught that it was about a "woman's right to choose." Isaac had agreed, until Ana convinced him otherwise. With ardor, she explained how the baby is not getting a choice, and how "choosing life" is very fulfilling. Being Catholic, Ana was vehemently opposed to abortion and found "pro choice" to be a clever way of being "pro death" or "anti life."

Becky and Travis were good people, and they listened. Once he established that he was there to advise and listen, rather than lecture or demean, Isaac realized he'd need not fulminate or preach on this day.

"So, are you just here to convince us to have the baby?" Travis interrupted, after a few minutes.

Isaac was not sure how to answer that, as sure, this was the overall idea, but as this was only the second time he'd met Travis, he didn't want to be a knave.

"No, not really," Isaac mumbled. "Just talk, listen and explain how much I care about you guys and how happy I am to have known Becky."

"Are you leaving?" Becky asked.

"No, not yet, but eventually…"Isaac answered, leaving the question open for the future. He tried to sound confident, and thankfully it seemed to work, as those questions ceased.

"We're keeping it, bro, don't worry, all right?" Travis said with a smile.

Isaac was overjoyed, and now felt odd about how hard he was trying to convince these two. He should have realized that one story from Becky about a moment of emotional rhetoric from Travis would not lead to an ignominious decision they'd regret for the rest of their lives. These folks cared more about personal responsibility than convenience.

Isaac was hesitant to inform them of his future plans. Before he departed, he felt such an uplifting conversation, perhaps their last, shouldn't end any ambiguity, so Isaac informed the couple of his thoughts on *his* future.

He didn't give them the "full version" obviously, but did tell Travis and Becky that he was unsure if he would be around much longer. When they asked why and when he might move on, Isaac offered little further information other than "family" and "if I am going to leave, it will be in the next few weeks." This was as much information as he could or would relay.

And with that, the subject briefly changed back to Travis and Becky, but it appeared all were on the same respectful wavelength. Isaac was not in position to foretell what their ultimate decision on the baby would be, or how their lives would transpire; he simply figured this chapter in his life was now complete. The three wished each other well, and though it was not the warmest good-bye, considering how friendly he and Becky had been, it would have been daft for Isaac to push farther into their lives or bid Becky adieu any longer.

18

Knoxville's Jewish community was not as small as you'd think for a southern Appalachia town. The school had an immensely popular and successful Jewish men's basketball coach, via Boston and Milwaukee, and though the campus lacked a Hillel Jewish Center, there were two synagogues to the southwest of the city. Knoxville also had a Jewish Day School, a nearby Chabad House, a chapter of Hadassah, Jewish Community Center on the Westside, as well as a "Jewish Alliance" to represent the interest of Jewish Knoxvillians.

Wanting to get away from campus and uninterested in "The Alliance" group, Isaac sought a rabbi's advice on his current state, even before contacting his wife. He had done this while the two were dating, as well as during their engagement, when they were pondering marriage and child rearing, so this was a piquant option.

Isaac was not embarrassed about this endeavor, nor did he think Ana would mind his going to temple first. In fact, she'd probably find it preferable that he sort matters out and then come to her with a coherent "plan." That's the way Mr. and Mrs. Hyde operated best.

The city of Knoxville's Jewish population grew from 766 Jews in 1948 to an estimated 1,800 60 years later with close to ninety-five percent being "professionals." Many were not native Knoxvillians, but had moved down to work in the growing medical center, the science labs at nearby Oak Ridge or the University.

A website Isaac once perused on Jewish history in eastern Tennessee claimed Knoxville "has been a microcosm of the demographic changes that have swept through the Jewish South over the last several decades."

And additionally it noted, "While these changes have decimated many small Jewish communities across the South, Knoxville has thrived as it has become an educational, medical, and research hub."

Despite never numbering more than 1,000 until the 1970s, Knoxville's Jewish community seemed strong, which made sense, as any ethno-religious "minority" group would naturally grow tighter. Even when the city had around 750 Jews six decades ago, Knoxville supported those two congregations, along with a JCC and a Jewish Federation, now deemed the "Alliance." As the size of the Jewish community grew over the last half century, it seemed its activity and its future prospects likewise augmented. The influence of Knoxville's Jewish community was well beyond its numbers, as in many other communities.

To speak with a rabbi, Isaac decided it would be most prudent to attend services on a Saturday, and seek him out, rather than just showing up on a weekday unannounced. There was no "confession" in Judaism, so generally, appointments needed to be arranged, unless you pulled the rabbi aside quickly after prayer on the Sabbath to schedule a short meeting. And that was usually pretty intrepid and frowned upon, especially on Saturdays.

Isaac attended a service at Temple Heska Amuna, on the city's west side that Saturday morning. Overall, it was no different than any of the weekly Sabbath, high holiday or conservative Jewish services he had taken the family to in New Jersey or attended with Ana or his parents in Maryland, Arizona or Indiana. Isaac supposed the only physical differences were the size of the temple, which was larger and older, and the people, who seemed quite pious for a non-Orthodox crowd, perhaps since there was no Orthodox shul in Knoxville.

Clad in fine southern garb, many also spoke with a refined southern tongue, being educated Jews, northern transplants and ardent Zionists, some of whom had dwelled in this part of the country for well over a century after emigrating from the "Old Country." Never forget, despite strict Baptists abounding there seemingly since time immemorial, the first American Jews came mostly to the south; to places like Knoxville, New Orleans, Birmingham, Atlanta, Memphis, Jackson, Savannah and especially Charleston, South Carolina.

Speaking of Charleston, pre-20th century Jewish history, was legendary. Isaac knew that the vast majority of the first Jews in America, before the great wave from Eastern Europe in the early 1900s, had originally settled in the south. Coastal Charleston was the Jerusalem or Prague/Warsaw/Kiev of its time.

The earliest record of a Jew in Charleston occurred in 1695, and seven years later numerous Jews voted at a general election. The Jewish community at Charleston received a large influx during the years 1740-41, when many Jews left the Georgia colony and flocked northward to South Carolina. The first synagogue established at Charleston was founded in 1750, mainly by Portuguese Jews, then German Ashkenazi Jews. The Jewish community was soon very prosperous, even before the American Revolution, with several Jews gaining financial distinction.

During the actual Revolutionary War, the Jews of Charleston distinguished themselves by their patriotism and devotion to the cause of independence, fighting in the battlefield. South Carolina was also the first place in the western world to elect a Jew to public office, and was the birthplace of Reform Judaism in the Americas.

By 1800 there were nearly 2,000 Jews in Charleston, which was more than in any other town, city, or place in North America. Charleston remained the unofficial capital of North American Jewry until about 1830, when an increasing number of German Jews emigrated to America and settled in the north-east, particularly in New York City, eventually surpassing the Jewish community in Charleston.

There were numerous prominent Jews in the South from the very beginning into today. As a military historian, Isaac was most familiar with Judah Benjamin, the first Attorney General of the Confederacy, their 2nd Secretary of State, and 3rd Secretary of War. And Tennessee, especially its eastern portion, had always been sympathetic to so-called "minorities." After Reconstruction, the Volunteer State was respected as "the most consistently competitive political system in the south… with blacks voting freely."

In the late 20th and early 21st century, Knoxville and its surrounding areas had a fair share of Jewish doctors, optometrists, lawyers, architects, and some engineers with the Tennessee Valley Authority, as well as a number of scientists doing secret work at Oak Ridge National Laboratories. Like many communities, there were Jewish businessmen or "merchants" in dry goods and apparel, jewelry, pawn shops, plumbing, beauty supplies, home furnishings and scrap yards. There was also a kosher-style deli, bakery, and food wholesaler.

Temple "Heska Amuna" literally translates to "Strongholders of the Faith." It was the second oldest congregation in Eastern Tennessee, established in 1890. Prior to the temple's opening, its members were affiliated with Temple Beth El, built during the Civil War. There had been some quarrels over religiosity, with Amuna's new members looking for a more traditional temple than the Reform Beth El.

Isaac had read up on the two congregations before deciding upon from which to visit and seek advice. He learned:

Beth El's membership swelled from 45 members in 1940 to 150 in 1962, which prompted the congregation to build a bigger synagogue in 1957 out in the suburbs west of Knoxville, where many Jewish businesses were located. Soon, both the JCC and Heska Amuna followed. Today, Beth El has 240 members, and has been served by a female Rabbi for the past decade.

In 1900, Heska Amuna had a synagogue, a full-time rabbi and 75 members. In 1957, it had 204 members, as compared to just 120 at Beth El. In 1960, Heska built a new synagogue just down the street from Beth El's new temple. That same year, the congregation voted to join the Conservative Movement, officially leaving Orthodox Judaism behind, after having long ago introduced such changes as mixed gender seating. Heska Amuna has had a very ephemeral rabbinate, with none staying in Knoxville for very long.

Isaac then learned that Rabbi Max Zucker, who led the congregation during most of the 1960s, was its longest serving rabbi since the early 1900s. They now have 250 members, including some from small towns outside Knoxville, and maintain the same rabbi since 2004.

And that was the rabbi who Isaac would see.

Rather than being churlish and asking the Rabbi that day, Isaac made sure to smile and introduce himself upon exiting the temple when the rabbi and cantors stand by the door to acknowledge congregants. He knew that in a small congregation such as Heska, his face might stand out. That was a good thing.

The following day, a beautiful Sunday in late February, Isaac crafted a straightforward email to Rabbi Levin. It stated:

Dear Rebbe Levin {Isaac did his best to inform the Rabbi he knew his Yiddish, thus potentially actuate his request more rapidly):

I wanted to introduce myself. For the past few months, I have resided here in Knoxville as a graduate student at the University of Tennessee. My family lives in New Jersey, where I have also lived for the past two decades. I chose to spend this school year in Knoxville in order to obtain my Masters Degree, so as to improve my professional lot back home. Though most of my experiences have been positive, and I only have a few months to go, I am having difficulties being away from those I love. Without seeming insolent, I was hoping I might have a few moments, at some point soon, to discuss my feelings with you.

Not wanting to rush into any decision, either way, that might come back to haunt me down the road, I believe a rabbi's wisdom is necessary at this point. My wife concurs.

I look forward to hearing from you about this "requisition."

Cordially,

Isaac J. Hyde

It wasn't perfect. Isaac felt it did not flow very well, but at the same time, he needed be somewhat terse, which was never his strength. This was affable and would do for now. He pressed "send" from his computer.

19

Monday morning, fewer than 24 hours after he submitted the email, Isaac's phone rang. Rabbi Levin was on the line. Isaac was impressed that his email was returned via phone; this meant the Rabbi was interested in listening. They arranged to meet at the temple at 4pm that afternoon. Isaac prepared some questions in his mind, so as to maximize his time with the rabbi.

Without beating around the bush, Isaac wanted the rabbi's insight as to what he should do between now and mid-May: stay in Knoxville and finish what he started, or go home to assist his family in a "turbulent" time. He decided he'd simply ask that very question.

Rabbi Levin's office was small and stacked with books on Judaism: biblical, political, social, familial, and so on. Isaac scanned over them, noting how many dealt with "raising kids Jewish" and "Jewish marriages." Few, if any, dealt with inter-faith marriage. This worried him. No matter what affiliation a rabbi or temple had, they were, as Isaac had heard before, "in the business of growing Jewish families." To the more reformed or secular, just being Jewish, not how much you know or care about the religion's unparalleled history of struggle, survival and determination, was more important than anything. As long as they married other "cultural Jews," even those who had never had a Bar Mitzvah, could not read Hebrew, couldn't identify any history aside from the basics of Hanukkah and Passover and cared nothing about Israel or Jewish values, they were venerated more than someone like Isaac, who knew and cared about all those matters deeply, but had married a "gentile."

This had always puzzled Isaac. Ana understood, respected, and cared more about Judaism than nearly any Jewish woman he knew, but that she was not Jewish and his children were not being raised 100% Jewish (they still attended services and knew their Judaism more than most Jews) made her "less Jewish" than the secular mothers who'd begrudgingly take their offspring to high holiday services twice per year, and that was it. This licentious behavior and hypocritical attitude was not lost on Ana, nor Isaac, but she never made her views public. Thankfully, as time went on, at least their parents understood how pure their mission was in comparison.

But would Rabbi Levin? This was one reason Isaac had chosen a conservative rabbi over a reform or even orthodox. The Orthodox, though the most knowledgeable in Judeo-Christian values, the old and new testaments and their connections, could still be cantankerous when it came to inner-faith marriages. The Reform, though "liberal," lacked knowledge, thus were wrongly suspicious of non-Jews entering into the covenant of "G-d's Chosen People." Same with the Reconstructionist Jews, the more modern radical movement that holds "contemporary Western secular morality has precedence over Jewish law and theology." Isaac disagreed 100%. Therefore, rightly or wrongly, Isaac felt he might find a middle ground with the conservative rabbi, who was well-received by those who knew him.

From the beginning, this was not the case. Rabbi Levin was curt and all business. Perhaps he frowned upon Isaac just requesting a meeting as a newcomer, but Isaac did not sense any of the compassion he had seen from the priests he and Ana had encountered in years past, nor most of the rabbis. The inter-faith marriage topic was not even broached as that was immaterial to the help Isaac was seeking. He knew rabbis were not trained psychologists but they were very well-trained in advising Jewish couples. Isaac and Ana were basically one of those, as Ana considered herself a "completed Jew," and surely Isaac was a full-blooded Jew seeking advice. The rabbi didn't seem to care. In fact, he visibly blanched when Isaac explained the children were being raised more Catholic than Jewish. Rabbi Levin didn't care for Isaac's explanation. This was presumably of little interest to him, especially because Isaac was an ephemeral resident of Knoxville.

After Isaac pressed for just a modicum of advice, Rabbi Levin, as torpid as Isaac could imagine a religious figure, rubbed his beard, leaned forward and spoke his piece.

"Well, as I see it, you have two options," he said in a measured voice, akin to a politician or lawyer.

"You can stay," as he pointed at the floor. "Or you can go" as he pointed toward the office door, letting out something of an insincere chuckle.

Though Isaac knew the Rabbi was just opening up his editorial comments, he realized why he was not paying for this psycho-analysis.

"I am of the opinion you must do what's best for your family," his erudite analysis continued. "And that comes from your heart."

Isaac was about to nod, shake the rabbi's hand, thank him and depart, when Rabbi Levin grabbed his knee.

"Son, a marriage involves not only a man and a woman, but G-d and your relationship with him," he explained. "You're living for the Diety, not yourself. What would G-d choose for your path?"

Many would have been bewildered by such a conundrum, but Isaac, who had heard this before from clergy and even Ana, knew what it meant. He smiled. Rabbi Levin smiled back, knowing that Isaac was enlightened enough to comprehend the meaning behind his words, even if vague.

Isaac again grinned, now shook the rabbi's hand, offered a heartfelt thanks, and departed. He called Ana immediately.

Ana, who was barely privy to any of the thoughts ruminating in Isaac's head the past few days since Lauren's departure, answered, out of breath. Isaac knew he'd caught her at an inopportune time and said he'd call back. Ana, perhaps sensing in Isaac's voice that it was important said, "No, no, just give me two minutes and I'll call you right back."

Like Isaac, Ana was timely and considerate; when she said two minutes, she meant it. This had been an area early in their dating lives that endeared Isaac to her. He could not imagine marrying someone wishy-washy or lax with time.

The cell phone rang.

"Baby, I have news," Isaac announced, as though he was a news anchor.

"Yes, dear," Ana asked, still out of breath.

"I'm coming home," Isaac stated very proudly.

"Cute, honey, when?" Ana said happily.

"Well, I have a few loose ends to tie up, so it may be a little more than a week."

"Spring break is that soon?" Ana wondered.

Isaac realized Ana was not her sagacious self, and therefore did not understand that he meant permanently.

"No, for good," he announced with pride. "I'm coming home for good!"

There was a three to four second pause and a snicker. Then Ana continued.

"Did you finish the program early...or get kicked out"

Isaac heard Ross laugh, or perhaps that was Lauren.

Isaac's energy dropped about 50%. Though it could have been worse since they had yet to discuss this decision as they often did most others, Isaac was still miffed by the mocking tone and lack of excitement from Ana and whomever was in the car with her.

"No, I thought about it, consulted a rabbi, and have made the necessary adjustments to end the program early," he explained nervously.

"Oh, Isaac, this is a lot to digest. Can I ask you something," Ana said delicately. "Will you be getting the Masters Degree before you leave?"

Isaac suddenly felt his heart drop as he pulled to the side of the undulating road back to Knoxville proper, gazing at the foothills of the Smokies to his right. He was dumbfounded that Ana was now putting the academic side over family. Maybe he should have asked her first? No, of course he should have, even though nothing was at all final.

"Well, not necessarily, though that angle is still pending. I did it for you and the kids, and the Rabbi also felt it was best, don't you?"

Again, silence from Ana's end. Had he come across Machiavellian?

"Isaac, let's talk about this tonight, ok?" she requested.

Isaac was glad no decisions were official, and knowing Ana, realized she was not that upset, but also was not going to "give in to him" and his emotional ideas right then and there. This was fine. He agreed to chat later, when in a more relaxed state.

20

By the time Isaac got through two lengthy calls with Ana about the "situation," it was nearly March. The semester had but nine weeks remaining, the weather was warming and spring break was two weeks away. If he were to leave for good, doing it at spring break time was best. Anything later made no sense. What made the most sense to Isaac was returning home, for his sanity and for the future well-being of his family. Ana, however, didn't necessarily see it that way.

It may have been the intellectual elitist in her, or maybe something different, but she was more in favor of Isaac staying to finish his academic pursuits. This was understandable. After all, Isaac had already completed most of the term, and she had been through a lot of alone time, so she figured he should finish – for his sake and hers. And if Ana felt she could deal with the home front, should he stop her? With all the stress up north, it would be far more salubrious down on his own in G-d's country; thus, Isaac accepted Ana's "offer" on its initial basis. He knew this was not going to be the end of the debate, however.

Within a week, a third conversation, so as to hopefully finalize Isaac's plan, took place. This was just a school week prior to Isaac's March break, and Isaac reminded Ana at the onset of a Tuesday night phone call that they needed to "resolve" this matter, as it was driving him crazy.

Ana understood. She said the decision was his entirely. This was exactly what Isaac did not want to hear. Knowing Ana was acting as Ana the psychologist, not the wife, he was angered. Why she was apparently pursuing schadenfreude right now, of all times, truly angered Isaac. This tactic was his pet peeve with his wife of nearly two decades. To use this with her patients or even children was one thing, but with a serious familial and spousal matter was unacceptable, in Isaac's view. He told Ana that. Fortunately, she knew this and later spoke to Isaac as Ana the Wife, not the Shrink.

But she still believed he should finish what he started in Knoxville, and Ana assured Isaac she'd be fine. She said Ross was doing better, "though he's crossing the days off his calendar until you return."

"And Lauren is back into a routine," she added. "She's not going to parties until the summer, and comes home after school by herself or with a female friend to study most days."

Isaac felt at ease.

"She also plans to try out for the junior varsity tennis team in a few weeks, once the weather warms up," Ana claimed.

Though Isaac had recommended it, he still chuckled. Lauren, like her mother, was not incredibly athletic. She had beauty and brains, but not brawn. Isaac and Ross were the athletes.

"She's been practicing against the wall at school," Ana said happily.

Isaac tried to avoid being vituperative, in case Lauren was eavesdropping or Ana was sensitive to the matter.

"Um, she doesn't play," he said.

Isaac had hit balls with Lauren and knew she grasped the basics, though she'd shown little interest in the game Isaac still enjoyed from time to time with his guy friends.

Ana explained what Isaac knew: that not only was this a fantastic way to keep Lauren out of trouble, but also that the freshmen girls' tennis team at a suburban New Jersey high school was not exactly filled with future Martina Navratilovas.

This was all quite true. And in the scheme of things, was good news, but not imperative information, so Isaac surreptitiously changed the topic.

"Ana, are you sure you can maintain things for another two months?" Isaac asked.

"Whether I can or not, I have to. You just worry about your Masters and leave this to me," she said.

Clearly he knew she was, without even having Ana affirm this.

And so that was basically that.

Isaac wasn't disappointed, just confused. But he'd make the best of it, enjoying his upcoming week at home, then the return to solitude in Knoxville for the "home stretch." He'd ended his "relationship" with Becky and Travis, so distractions, if any, would be minimal.

21

Saint Patrick's Day and the first 70-degree day in Eastern Tennessee since early November meant it was time for Isaac to return north to see his family, where it was sleeting and in the mid 30s. Being fascinated by weather patterns, and not adverse to wintry weather while it was technically still winter, Isaac looked forward to his ride up. He always did, but knowing this was the second to last time going north – and last time whereupon he'd return – he cherished this pleasant journey a tad bit more.

As Isaac drove north and crossed into the Commonwealth of Virginia, he let his mind slip into the joys of some NCAA tournament college basketball on the AM radio. He was a huge sports fan, but with life eating at him lately, athletics has taken a distant backseat. Baseball season was not yet quite underway, so this was the first time Isaac had lent his full attention to the diversion that is sports. As the signal faded in and out like the sporadic sleet which was now flurries as he moved through Bristol, Isaac was content.

Then the phone rang. It was Ana. Was she calling to tell him she'd changed her mind? Or to lecture him? Or just to perhaps ask when he'd arrive home?

Isaac was panicking for some odd reason, and that was telling.

But there was no reason to be concerned. Ana indeed did want to find out his estimated time of arrival. Though Isaac, as usual, sought detours, he didn't want Ana to get out of her gourd with anticipation, so he said "seven hours." That was a conservative estimate, as he could do it in six flat, but wanted time for a potential stop near some Civil War sites in Virginia, should he choose to cut through the Richmond or Fredericksburg area, then north to DC.

Though Isaac was a bit less relaxed due to such "time constraints," he knew these were not set in stone, so he proceeded north along lovely I-81. This spring ride presented Isaac with a third distinct viewing of the eastern backbone of Virginia's marvelous Blue Ridge mountain chain. He'd seen them in the lush green and blue of late August, the hard gray and black granite of winter and now the mixture of those two in early spring. Still, Isaac never tired of scanning the pastured valleys to the east, tumbling away in every direction, their grassy folds cradling the endless array of white farmhouses and red barns.

The farther north he went though, the more bleak and "wintry" the terrain, naturally. Temperatures were in the mid 40s, with partly cloudy skies, so Isaac detoured at the lovely mid-sized city of Roanoke and hopped on the Blue Ridge Parkway, which ran jaggedly parallel through the enormous George Washington and Thomas Jefferson National Forest, headed for a rejoinder with the interstate near historic Lexington, Virginia. That was roughly a 50 mile journey, accomplished in 45 minutes easily on the interstate, but on the twisty, scenic Parkway, with average speeds of 40 and multiple viewpoints to stop at, Isaac knew 90 minutes was likely. It was now nearly 2pm, and with the recent daylight savings time, he had a good five hours of daylight left, so this was a no-brainer move. A stoppage at Civil War battlefields near Richmond or not, Isaac would still be home well before midnight. This being a Saturday, all was good.

As Isaac maneuvered onto the "BRP," he was in heaven: a panoply of rolling hills, forests, vast and mountainous terrain engulfed him. Though the wind picked up and ominous rain clouds beckoned on the horizon in all directions, Isaac could not care less. He took a few short hikes from lookout points down ridges toward the oak trees and dogwoods, enjoying every minute of it. Gazing out, Isaac fondly recalled recently reading that over 90% of America was still undeveloped, and that trees alone cover more than six times the area of all cities and towns in the country put together. An incredible 1.8 million acres of America's forests are remote, undeveloped or are designated as "wilderness areas," which prohibits future development. This has been the case for nearly a century. Isaac's skeptical mind couldn't help but scoff at how few people were around, considering the natural beauty of the area. The so-called environmentalists, often residing in overcrowded locales, tirelessly searching for the "last green spot," therefore rarely noticed the endless open spaces in our nation. They were nowhere to be seen on this pristine day. Apparently, demagoguery beats data, when it came to eco-alarmism.

After 50 of his 64 miles on this portion of the parkway – known to Isaac since there are mile posts every individual mile—had been covered, the skies opened up and rain pelted the Mazda furiously. The road was, naturally, hilly and windy; and though scenic, when a torrential downpour makes visibility no more than 15 feet, even Isaac was not enjoying his time. Further, with sun out of sight and gray all around, this was no passing storm. Isaac needed to move along at a 30 mile-per hour clip, and hopefully move through the final dozen miles until he hit the state highway to Lexington (and eventually the interstate) in about 25 minutes. Daylight was aplenty, but with the dark clouds, it looked more like dusk.

Isaac then realized, in the midst of this chaos, that he had some baggage exposed on the top of the car. He decided to get out and moor the boxes to the vehicle now, rather than later. Stepping out onto the road, Isaac realized this was no ordinary storm; this was brutal, and he was not imperturbable under such trying conditions. He studied wars, but did not fight in them, nor pretended he'd be good in those endeavors. In any event, Isaac secured his belongings, took a deep breath, and piled back into the car and began driving as methodically as ever. His car was also somewhat heavy with the extra luggage, which made driving a tougher struggle, especially at 3,000 feet elevation. Isaac then called Ana to tell her his predicament.

But Ana did not answer her cell phone, and no one picked up at home. No big deal though, as Isaac left a calm message on both phones and pressed on.

At about mile marker 56, the winds were so strong that Isaac had to hold on to the steering wheel with about as much strength as he could muster. "White knuckled driving," this surely was. And though he appreciated the "excitement" per se, Isaac also was looking forward to finishing these last few miles, descending down into Buena Vista, Virginia, then entering Lexington near the interstate.

There were no other cars in sight. And though the Blue Ridge Parkway is seldom straight for more than a mile, Isaac had not seen a car for at least 15 minutes. They had somehow bailed out, or who knows what. Isaac pressed on, now 2660 feet above sea level. He and the Mazda maneuvered through some debris, and when he saw mile marker 50 next to a sign that read "exit to Buena Vista: 4 miles," Isaac breathed a heavy sigh of relief. Overall, this would be one of his most memorable tours of the Parkway, but not for all the best reasons.

About two miles before the exit to the main roads, two diminutive flashing lights crossed the road in front of Isaac. Too small to be a car, it had a brown backside. This was clearly a deer. Though it was not dusk, the clouds and rain had made the sky look like the sun was setting for the day, and therefore deer were apparently out. This one was a few feet from Isaac by the time he could glean what in fact the figure was for certain. Isaac jolted the car left, where thankfully no one was coming, then back to the right, but he went too far and felt himself losing control, so he overcompensated and moved back to the right, then left, then right again, and eventually was off the road. Not knowing what was below, and how far down he might fall, Isaac slammed the brakes and plowed into some trees and other foliage.

22

Isaac was quite conscious and just a little shaken when he looked up to see raindrops covering his windshield, which was, thankfully, not cracked. He looked around the car to see nothing worse than bags and books tossed around. As he ran the wipers, he saw brush and tree limbs hanging atop his windows. By feeling his car's position, there was no doubt his car (and maybe his life) had been saved by the wet mud he had thrown his car into when he broke hard. Isaac gingerly opened his door and stepped out of the car into the pouring rain to survey and the damage around him.

For someone who had never really had any "exciting" car accidents, the scene looked preternatural: his car was nearly at a 45 degree angle, stuck into the muck, with shrubbery all around it. The back and sides, overall, looked fine. He was also a good 20 feet from the cliff's edge, which was a good thing, because a drop of nearly 500 feet awaited at that point. Isaac looked around, trying to think of what to do, when suddenly a car that had just driven past made a U-turn about 200 feet in the distance and drove toward him. It pulled up at road's edge and, flashlight in hand, a man and woman trotted in Isaac's direction.

Isaac, hailing from the northeast, was surprised that anyone would be decent enough to venture assistance especially in such weather. He wondered if he himself would have even been kind enough to help someone in need.

In any event, the middle-aged couple with the silver American style truck, asked him if he was okay.

Isaac, at best he could, affirmed.

"Well, we saw you swerving and then turn into this here ditch, so we figured we may as well check on you," the man said.

"I thank you kindly for that, I sure do," Isaac said in his most genteel voice.

"A deer?" the lady asked, as the rain pelted her.

"Seems that way," Isaac responded.

"Next time hit him," both said. Isaac laughed, but they did not. They were, of course, one hundred percent serious.

"OK, makes sense," said Isaac.

"Where ya' headed?" the man inquired.

Isaac was not sure if he needed to share all the details, so he said, "Home...New Jersey."

The couple looked quizzically.

"This was just a scenic detour," Isaac said with a smile, looking at the downpour from above.

They chuckled.

"It is a beautiful road no matter the weather, but with darkness or rain, it's not as easy to ride – then there's the deer," the man said, with a nod to his wife.

Isaac decided that even though the weather was brutal, he may as well be amicable.

"And so what brings you here?"

"Believe me or don't, this is actually a short cut to our house," he said, in a local's jargon.

Isaac pictured the map, the paucity of exits on the Parkway, and tried to figure out how that was possible, but did not press further. There were houses adjacent to the parkway, though not many. It was interesting, nevertheless.

"Yep, get our groceries and do other shopping in Lexington or BV, then hitch up here, and we're another 9 miles down to the south," he explained. "We were fixin' to do more, but with the rain, headed back."

Isaac thought that was really cool. Most of the houses off the BRP, since the road was maintained by the National Park Service, were immaculate, quiet and, like the adjacent land, capacious. But this was all immaterial now.

"You think you'll be able to get your vehicle out of the mud by yourself?" the gentleman asked, likely knowing Isaac, nor anyone, could do that on their own.

"I'm seriously doubting that, sir." Isaac answered quickly. He loved the wry sense of humor, charm and honesty of small town folks.

The man, whose name was Chuck – his wife was Shirley – went back to his car to retrieve some gloves and other implements, most of them foreign to Isaac.

After about ten parlous minutes of pulling, twisting, pushing and prodding, much of it with Shirley in the driver's seat and the men providing the muscle, the car was liberated from the earth and propelled itself onto the side of the road where it could rest on pavement. No cars were in sight. Despite it still only being 4:30pm, Isaac knew he'd gotten quite lucky.

Isaac offered Chuck and Shirley $20 for their troubles, but they naturally declined. These were good-natured folks, not run by greed or avarice. Isaac gave them his business card, and told them with sincerity that he'd take them to lunch if ever they were in the New York City area. They nodded, with both knowing they were not interested in the cesspool of Manhattan. There were at least two Americas, and thank goodness for that, Isaac thought. In fact, Isaac had spent the past seven months in a third America, perhaps in between his and Chuck's. That happy medium was more his speed, although he'd strongly consider Chuck and Shirley's over his in New Jersey. Isaac then watched their pick-up truck disappear around the next bend, off in the direction of some bucolic estate, and a simple American lifestyle.

23

As Isaac rolled along the final few miles, then carefully down the steep grade about 1500 feet into the Buena Vista area, and eventually across the highway to historic Lexington, he knew he'd have to get a hotel room for the night. The car very well might have been able to make it the final 400 miles on interstate 81, but it also could just as easily not. Tomorrow was Sunday, unfortunately, which meant most of the stores and auto shops would not open before 1pm. Thus, even with perfect timing and a "clean bill of health" for the Mazda, he'd be lucky to be on the road before 2 or 3pm, and not home until around 9 or 10pm on a Sunday night. Oh well, Isaac still had all week, and perhaps he could see some of the great historic sites and gorgeous outlying areas, including Washington and Lee University, as well as Virginia Military Institute of Lexington while in town.

Isaac, famished from the drive and ordeal, chowed down on a burger at some quiet local grille, It was now 6pm or thereabouts, and still mostly light. Further the rain has ceased, and the sun made an appearance for the final moments of daylight.

Isaac drove into the town proper, population 6,500, and gawked at the churches, museums and "history." It was wonderfully uplifting, spiritual and patriotic. He had an hour of daylight left, so he decided to use that for brief observation.

Ana called. Isaac realized he had not called her. That was bad, though the accident was surely an honest alibi.

But of course, Ana did not know about his travails.

"Hey, honey, how close are you? Into Pennsylvania yet?" she asked.

"Well, no. In fact, I won't be home until tomorrow…"

"Really?" Ana asked, peevishly.

"No, dear. I had a mishap, but am okay."

Silence on the other line.

"I'm okay," Isaac repeated.

"Isaac, were you on one of your historic detours?" Ana again asked in a jocular way.

"Sort of, well, yes," Isaac stammered. "I was on the Blue Ridge Parkway."

Ana took a deep breath. She knew that weather, danger or common sense would never cause her husband to abandon a potential scenic or historical adventure.

Isaac knew she was thinking this, too.

"Ok, well, out with it – what happened?" Ana asked.

"I was in an *accident*," Isaac made sure he used and emphasized that noun and not "mishap."

Ana was silent for a moment, then offered this empathetic sigh:

"Oh, are you okay?"

Obviously, Isaac was, or the call would have come from the police or local hospital. He told her that, in a kinder way.

Next Ana asked about the condition of the car. Isaac explained his plan to have it checked out before driving home. She calmly agreed.

And that was about it, thankfully. Isaac did not pick a time to return Sunday, but said he'd call with an update once he was on his way.

It was still daylight, the days longer now, so Isaac figured he should enjoy the rest of the afternoon in such a wondrous and historic place, wind down, seek out the hotel situation, enjoy a semi-early night's sleep, then set about finding any mechanic who'd be open before noon. Sunday Church is a big deal in this part of Virginia. He was a long way, culturally and geographically, from the Arlington/Alexandria area outside DC, much less Richmond in the center's Piedmont Region, as well as the coastal Tidewater region. As states go, Virginia wrote the book on diversity in every avenue.

Isaac parked his car next to a historic marker. He expected to read about Civil War history – Grant, Jackson, even Lee – but no, this predated those fellows by a little bit. The marker was dedicated to none other than Sam Houston.

The man, among much else, partnered with Andrew Jackson in the War of 1812 and, briefly fought in the Civil War, before pneumonia caused him to become a *hors de combat*. Unbeknownst to even Isaac however, this Texan was actually born on "Timber Ridge" in 1792, just north of Lexington. Isaac was aware that Houston, though a Tennessean and supporter of Jacksonian democracy, still listed his political party as "Independent" in the Antebellum South. He is still the only person in American history to serve as governor of two different states — first Tennessee and then Texas. The latter occurred during the Texas War for Independence, where he was technically the first and only "president of a foreign state." Houston was later senator from Texas – the state he essentially procured for the United States -- during the Mexican-American War, and the state's current largest city was named in his honor prior to that, in 1837.

Sam Houston convinced President Jackson that "Tejas," as it was then known, was worth annexing to the USA. The state's admission was controversial, as it threatened to tear the delicately-preserved senatorial balance between free and slave states asunder. Nonetheless, a state whose people had patterned their revolution against the "Tejanos" after our own American Revolution some sixty years prior, were not to be stopped. The Lone Star State went on to aid, and "repay its debt" to the US in its war with Mexico a decade later. This nationalism and dedication to service among Texans continues today.

Then there were some Civil War-era anecdotes Isaac knew a bit about, yet still found very interesting:

Sam Houston was something of a polemicist.

Though a slaveowner, and by 1859, head of a Southern state, Houston was a "southern Unionist." He therefore opposed the secession of Texas from the Union. In 1860, he warned of "the sacrifice of countless millions of treasure and hundreds of thousands of lives" in the Civil

War. He added that he doubted the South would win, because "The North is determined to preserve this Union."

Despite Houston's warning, Texas seceded from the United States in February 1861 and joined the Confederate States of America on March 2, 1861. Texas's secession was powerful enough to replace the state's "northern sympathizing" governor. Houston did not resist, and he was evicted from his office in March 1861 for "refusing to take an oath of loyalty to the Confederacy."

He wrote a long treatise that, broken down to apercus, noted:

"In the name of the constitution of Texas, which has been betrayed by the Convention, I refuse to take this oath."

A lifelong insomniac, Houston finally drifted into perpetual sleep two years after the cessation of hostilities in 1867, uttering "Texas, Texas." In a state whose population was under 40,000 when it achieved statehood well under two centuries ago, to its current boasting of 25 million residents, Sam Houston remains a favorite son.

Isaac felt Houston was a brave soul to refuse to "soldier his state" into battle. He was the antithesis of Robert E. Lee in that way, but equally admirable in some circular historic fringe of great Americans. And clearly this obduracy was well-intentioned and proven correct. Four years and 260,000 confederate lives (620,000 counting both sides) later, the South was again part of these United States. The first 12 years after the war, ten of which Houston was not alive to see, witnessed the madness and debauchery of a bungled Southern Reconstruction. Unlike Andrew Johnson, Rutherford B Hayes, the former confederate leaders and perhaps President Lincoln, Mr. Houston likely understood that freeing slaves was only a small part of the long battle; bringing the ex-slave population into "the civilized world," especially in the South, was an arduous task. It was so monumentally impossible in fact, that one could argue that the matter remained unresolved for a full century after true "disenfranchisement" occurred when the country moved forward into its Industrial Age, leaving the issues of the Civil War in limbo for decades to come and future generations to tackle.

And that was ol' Sam Houston. As the sun set, Isaac enjoyed the recollection. He figured he'd save Lee, Jackson and the universities for tomorrow while he undoubtedly waited for his car.

24

Isaac procured a room at the Days Inn. It was not your typical Days Inn, in that it felt more like a sprawling country motel, with outdoor grounds, patios and colonial architecture.

Lexington's population is just under 7,000 denizens. First settled in 1777, it sits about 60 miles east of the West Virginia border, and is the county seat of little Rockbridge County. No doubt its primary economic activity stems from higher education as well as tourism, mainly historical, most notably the Robert E. Lee Chapel and Stonewall Jackson house. Both are buried in Lexington. The city sits at the crossroads of historic US Routes 11 and 60; and now the more modern highways, Interstates 64 and 81.

Isaac read some of this before he turned in for the night, enjoying some of the national news on TV he'd missed the past 24 hours. Temps were slowly dropping outside, into the low 30s and sleet was expected before noon Sunday. "Perfect," Isaac said sardonically, as he shut his eyes.

Morning was bleak. The town was desolate. Everything seemed closed, so Isaac went over to Washington and Lee University, about a mile down the road from his hotel, where he was able to find some hearty souls milling about in the cold, including the crew team practicing. This was the southern aristocracy at its "finest." It was a site to see, with the beautiful buildings and statuary all around. And this was Washington & Lee; he had yet to move over to Virginia Military Institute (VMI) – the "West Point of the South" -- whose campus was adjacent to Wash and Lee.

After a few more glances at the campus, it was 11am, so Isaac figured that at least one of the body shops or auto car places might be opening up; therefore he rolled back into town, figuring he could walk back to the campus areas later.

The Stonewall Jackson museum in downtown Lexington did not open until 1pm, which was quite disappointing, since the site is the only house Jackson ever owned, and now a museum dedicated to the general's life and times.

James Robertson Jr., a Civil War historian at Virginia Tech University, wrote this of Jackson in his epoch 1000 page 1997 biography.

"Military genius and religious devotion are not common traits among mankind. When one individual possesses both seemingly incompatible qualities, he stands alone on a high pedestal that is extraordinary to some, enigmatic to others."

It was also noted that Jackson's faith permeated every action of his adult life. Historians report that he began each task by offering a personal blessing, and he completed every duty by returning thanks to G-d. He also did not read or discuss secular subjects on Sunday.

As a Jew who admired the Orthodox that felt the similarly about Saturday – the seventh day – Isaac surely admired this, even though he knew Jackson, like so many other great American leaders of the past, would be vilified by today's secular masses for such a traditional outlook.

Sadly for the South, death ultimately removed Jackson from the scene at the apogee of military fame; his success was enjoyed by no other Civil War figure, sans perhaps Grant, Lee and Sherman. That passing, at a high point in Rebel success (the stunning victory of May 1863 in Chancellorsville), was considered the greatest loss suffered by the wartime south. Robert E. Lee so noted this. Jackson was so revered, that his likeness graced the most expensive confederate note: a $500 bill made in Richmond.

Isaac was disappointed time and day would not permit his visit to this historical site, but in actuality, it gave him time to deal with the more urgent issue of his car.

Isaac did not pass any car places open until at least noon, and most were actually 1pm. He decided to hit up the library at Washington and Lee, thus killing three birds with a single stone: using the internet (since the public library was also closed until 1pm), escaping the outside chill for inside warmth, and seeing more of the campus. He trekked back up, parked, walked across a picturesque bridge, through the leafless trees and around some incredible colonial style buildings, then past a magnificent statue of Lee, fittingly atop a hill in front of the stately library. Upon entering the building, aptly called the "Lee Library," Isaac located the myriad modern computer kiosks which naturally looked out of place in a historic building. He learned that the only car repair place that seemed open was about three miles outside of town, called "Mike's." Isaac called to assure himself of this and there was no answer, but the recording did say "open 10am to 5pm Sundays." He decided to give it a try. If anything, there'd likely be no crowd and perhaps it would be cheaper.

Isaac carefully drove up into the scenic vista adjacent to Lexington, still within the city limits, and searched for the address to "Mike's Foreign and Domestic Car Care." All he found were houses, many quite run down. This was the impoverished Appalachia, and just a small part of it. Isaac knew from factual reports and statistics that most people in these environs were far more indigent than nearly anyone in the urban US ghettos. It was really not even close, especially in terms of material possessions. The difference was that these people, for whatever reason, were completely ignored by the mainstream media. Additionally, they had fewer, if any, social services, welfare centers or "interest groups" nearby, and no freshly stocked grocery store in walking distance. They surely had no fancy shoes nor big screen televisions. They had family, land and likely religion. They were most assuredly "self employed," to proud to ask for a handout anyway. These were, in Isaac's estimation, Forgotten Americans, but still represented the ideals of this nation.

All these thoughts notwithstanding, Isaac watched the addresses go by and only saw houses and trailers, no businesses, and surely no signs for "Mike's." He drove past signs of steady civilization, grandparents dozing in wicker chairs on their verandahs, eyeing the "stranger" in their midst. He came to an intersection labeled "Turnpike Rd" at the very edge of town and decided to go no farther. In a circumspect nature, Isaac calmly flipped a 180 in the Mazda and heard the sloshing sound of all the mud, then began to drive very slowly back, looking very carefully address by address....and Eureka! He found number 8204. Only it was a small, white rundown clapboard home just like most of the others. But upon more careful inspection, there was a garage with a rusty orange sign indicating this was, in fact, "Mikes Foreign and Domestic Car Care."

Isaac pulled halfway up the driveway so as not to alarm anyone, walked over and rapped on the side door of the garage. No answer. He tried again without response, and at that point, it being 11:30am, Isaac was about ready to move back into town and declare this morning a total loss. Then a woman came trotting out of the house and in a mildly friendly but concerned way asked Isaac if he needed help. Isaac pointed to his car and explained how he came upon Mike's. The woman appeared confused and told Isaac that they usually only assist in "special projects" with their "associates and vendors" but that Mike would "gladly take a peek." Isaac, with his abundant travel and cultural experiences, realized he should have figured both would be the case. He drove his car into the garage and awaited Mike.

Mike arrived a minute later, and appeared just as Isaac expected: corpulent, bearded, donning overalls and quite genuine. He took one look and said "where'd ya' get all this mud?" Isaac explained, just as he had to Ana yesterday evening and Mike's wife a few moments ago. Mike grunted. He walked around to the back of the vehicle to size up that situation, made some joke about the back looking clean, then got under the car to peer up into the engine. Mike laughed and reminded Isaac there was a ton of mud.

"But the good news is, it's only mud," he said. "I can get most of it out, but it'll take an hour or two, maybe more."

Unlike the erroneous stereotype films have of a small town mechanic, that's all Mike said. He did not say "it'll cost you" or name some ridiculous price. Isaac knew he would not. Mike was a good, honest man trying to help a fellow American in need. It was that simple. When Isaac sat down on an old wooden chair in the musty garage to wait, he asked Mike what he'd need for the job, money-wise. Mike, unlike some acrimonious repairmen, simply told him he'd see how long it took, then they could make a deal. Enough said.

It was quite nippy in the heatless garage, but Mike, working steadily at removing the muck from the Mazda, did not seem to care, therefore Isaac said nothing. Instead he conversed with Linda, Mike's wife. She happened to be a native of New York, though from the small western New York town of Brockport. Mike was a native Virginian, from Staunton, another historic city about 35 miles up I-81 from Lexington.

Many folks Isaac knew would have little to say to these people, but he was different. When his colleagues talked history, though he did not always agree with their invidious comparisons, he participated in productive discourse; when they talked about anything else like movies, music or television shows, he had little to say. The folks he'd met in Knoxville and people like Mike and Linda offered similar tastes to Isaac in food, sports, travel, family values, and likely politics. It was refreshing. The two hours, though cold and dreary, flew by, as Mike finished hosing off the Mazda and removed as much residue as was humanly possible. Though 20% definitely remained, Isaac was thrilled, told Mike so, and then took a photo of Mike in front of the vehicle for Ana to see later.

Though Mike had a computer and phone set up, he could not take plastic, and Isaac had no checks on him. Embarrassingly, Isaac had only $14 in cash. Mike, who was not a young man, had worked two solid hours. Fourteen dollars would be an insult, so should Isaac take his address and tell him he'd send him cash or check? He figured Mike would trust him, and Isaac would pay as soon as he returned. He was that kind of guy. But if Isaac suggested such an option, he mused that Mike might feel the man from the north was attempting to purloin the auto service. Stereotypes of "Yankees" and especially New Yorkers were rampant in the south, and often for good reason. Yes, Isaac and Mike had "bonded," but would Mike be perturbed if Isaac suggested he leave today without paying a dime?

Isaac worried for no reason. Mike was clearly no knave. Isaac explained the situation to him, and the considerate gentleman asked how much cash Isaac had on him. Isaac embarrassingly told him he had only the 14 dollars. Mike snickered a bit, but agreed that was fine. When Isaac told him he'd send whatever he liked in the mail no later than Tuesday, Mike said he should not bother. "It's totally fine, sir," he said with complete sincerity. Isaac was not surprised, thanked Mike profusely, yet still planned to send him at least $50 when he returned home. Two hours of manual labor at any auto body shop up would be well over $100, taxes and other "environmental fees" notwithstanding.

Isaac rolled away into a day that had suddenly turned brighter and more pleasant both figuratively and literally. Mike and Linda waved from their porch, and then went inside for lunch. Isaac arrived back into Lexington's main drag and saw the clock read 2:20pm. Did he have time to see VMI? No, not really; he had to get home, and if he departed now with minimal stops, he'd still pull into his driveway no earlier than 10pm, on a Sunday night no less.

Isaac had seen the wonders of Wash and Lee. And even though he had only glanced at the 142 year-old Lee Chapel at the center point of campus, he really had to move on now. He would also have to just park and walk by the Stonewall Jackson House and Museum, especially because of the steep $6 admission charge. Isaac's museum in New York City was free, as he mused museums should be. And the Manhattan museums, with much steeper overheads than the Jackson house, were often less expensive, due to state and municipal funding, which no doubt Stonewall's place lacked. Score one for the North, finally. But nonetheless, Isaac peered in and around the exterior of the building, then felt like he could "check it off" and "fall out" as the clock struck 1500 hours.

Clearly, Isaac would not being able to fully glimpse the Virginia Military Institute, the 170 year-old school with 1400 cadets/students. He did know that more than a dozen VMI graduates rose to the rank of general in the Confederate army, and that many served alongside Stonewall Jackson, even at Chancellorsville where Jackson was mortally wounded. A little over a year later in the war, Union forces burned the

Institute as part of the "Valley Campaigns of 1864." The destruction was so devastating that VMI temporarily held classes in Richmond, Virginia, until the school reopened six months after the war ended in October 1865.

As he moved through the streets toward I-81, Isaac carefully picked up a tourist brochure to learn that Virginia Military Institute is the oldest state-supported military college in the United States, and unlike any other state military college in America, all VMI students are military cadets.

Isaac moved north into a sun set that had just begun its slow descent into the late March sky. He had a good four hours of daylight left, perhaps more, but also a "good" six or seven hours of pavement ahead, so he moved rapidly. Isaac did so with reluctance, as the history and scenery around him was as impressive as anywhere in the United States. His family awaited, however, and truth be told, Isaac had driven this road numerous times, especially in the past few months.

Isaac pushed past Winchester, then into that very small portion of West Virginia before hitting the Maryland line near the tiny crossroads town of Hancock. He was across the Mason-Dixie and back into the north minutes later. Cracker Barrell then caught Isaac's eye near the Civil War town of Chambersburg, and he had chow for the first time in over eight hours. He hated to burn daylight, but he needed some nourishment which the restaurant's bounteous portions provided.

The Mazda did well all the way up those Pennsylvania hills before Isaac moved east, across the Lehigh Valley, and into New Jersey, arriving home safe and (mostly) sound just after 10:00 p.m.

25

The cliché tells us "home is where the heart is," and upon his entry and first hour back in New Jersey, Isaac would not disagree. Ross was all over him talking sports, wanting to do this or that, while Lauren, fresh from bonding with dad down in Knoxville, was inquisitive and gregarious. Ana was warm, genuine and understanding. Isaac hadn't been this happy in months. It made him long to come home sooner, or now, for good.

While waiting for Mike to repair his vehicle, Isaac had time to reflect on matters. The accident could have been worse. And if that were the case, where would that leave him and his family? He could not afford to even be incapacitated or unable to fulfill his role as father and husband. Why risk it all by being away and in less control of his life, even if just for a few more months?

It was a combination of said mindset and his "experiences" along the difficult road home that convinced Isaac, at least at this moment, that he needed to return home for good. He knew, especially after their recent conversation where she reassured her husband that she had things together up here, that Ana would initially dismiss the idea out of hand, but Isaac would try his best to help her understand his position.

And so, after a lovely night, the Hydes put their children to bed and then devoted the rest of the evening to some much-needed marital "relations."

In the morning, Lauren and Ross were proudly driven to school by their dad. Yes, even Lauren was not embarrassed. Ross was in ecstasy, overjoyed to have his dad with him. Isaac returned home to find Ana preparing to depart for work. She seemed distracted a bit, and was not her usual well-coiffed self.

"Is this casual Monday?" Isaac asked with a chuckle.

Ana faked a smile and ignored him.

Isaac, who at this point, had little to do but study and perhaps run some errands, glanced over and asked what was wrong.

Ana said "nothing."

But then she said, "Just some things at work." Isaac had become accustomed to Ana using terse replies when avoiding an issue.

She told Isaac they'd "talk tonight" about that matter, and his plans, and was then off.

As Isaac enjoyed a rare day of relaxation, he pondered what was eating at Ana. By the time she returned home, Isaac had already picked up the kids, taken them to the mall, bought a gift or two, and had a small snack, so that neither Ana nor he would not have to make dinner right away.

The family ordered Chinese Take Out, talked, laughed, reminisced, watched some TV, made plans for the rest of the week, then Ross went to bed and Lauren went to use the computer. Isaac couldn't wait any longer to discuss both issues with Ana. Being a gentleman, he let her start.

"Isaac, they gave me notice," she said with a stammer.

"Notice of…?" Isaac asked, knowing deep inside what she meant.

Ana explained that she was going to lose her job in three weeks, not due to performance, but rather "restructuring." She had been working at this practice for nearly a decade. They offered her four months' severance, but the decision was final.

Isaac took a deep breath, thought of his current life and job predicament and then let Ana continue, rather than interrupt. He knew this was a time simply to listen, not offer advice.

"So in mid-April I will be out of work. When do you return?" she asked.

"Second week of May, but …" Isaac tried to explain that he wanted to come back sooner, but Ana interrupted. Isaac also realized maybe he shouldn't come home now. This scenario was getting complicated.

Then Ana said something that came out of nowhere.

"Do you like Indiana?"

Isaac, miffed, answered honesty.

"Yes, love it, of course. Why?"

"Well, could you live there?" Ana asked.

"Could I, or would I?" Isaac replied.

Ana gave him a dirty look, but Isaac explained he definitely felt he could deal with life in Indiana, and to Ana's joy, he said he most certainly would enjoy life in the Hoosier State.

"And, uh, Isaac, what about your job here; you know, the one you've spent so much time in Tennessee trying to improve," Ana asked seriously.

"Well, now that I should have the Masters, it'll be easier to find employment anywhere, and hopefully with better pay," Isaac said confidently.

Ana ignored most of what Isaac said and focused on the word "should." She inquired as to why he used that particular term. Isaac explained that was part two of their conversation, and said maybe they should save that for tomorrow night. Ana chuckled. But Isaac was serious. His issue was in many ways "larger" than hers, so it would be rather overwhelming to solve that predicament the same night.

As to Indiana, Ana sensed Isaac was quite eager. It was almost as though the time in Knoxville and his personality made him long to move into the Heartland and away from the overcrowded coast and the many fatuous people residing there. Therefore, Ana told Isaac she planned to travel to Indiana for an April 1 interview with a clinic in Carmel, not far from her parents' residence in Westfield.

Her mom had the connection through a co-worker and, after Ana had emailed her resume, they had agreed to bring her in for an interview. The position would have similar responsibilities to Ana's current job, with only slightly less pay. Factoring in the much lower cost of living, even in Indiana's "wealthiest" suburbs north of Indianapolis, the Hydes would actually be better off, assuming Isaac could find reasonable work. The school system would be just as good, if not better. Of course, Ana would stay with her parents while in town, whose potential proximity would be a bonus if in fact she was offered she was offered the job in Indiana.

The issue now, at least in its initial phase, was set. Thankfully, both husband and wife were content, though they had not yet told the children. There was no need to, as the percentage chance of it all transpiring was fifty/fifty at best. It would be deleterious to surprise and excite the children if things did not work out.

Next, Isaac had to explain to Ana how and why he thought he should come home early. That she'd be away soon and busy might entice Ana to permit Isaac to leave the program. Not that he needed permission, but he also thought Ana might be "disappointed" if he left without consulting, much less withdrew from the program.

26

On Wednesday of his "break," Isaac took the mid-day subway into Manhattan. It was a reasonably pleasant day and unlike rush hour mornings, the subway was not crowded. After ambling around for awhile, Isaac basically stumbled upon his office/museum and decided there was no reason not to pay his colleagues a visit.

Upon entering the museum, much looked the same, but Isaac also noticed the crowds visiting were rather small. The Museum of Twentieth Century American History, despite being free to enter, had never drawn the crowds of other large Manhattan museums; yet still, it was dead in there, even for a Wednesday in March. He went down the back stairs to the office where the small museum staff, including his temporary replacement, resided from 9am-5pm weekdays. Two of the four folks were out to lunch, one out sick, leaving just his co-worker, Dave, in what they playfully called "the dungeon," due to the lack of windows and its basement locale. Dave looked up from his E-bay bidding, happy to see Isaac.

"How's it been going, man?" Isaac asked, looking around the office that seemed as if nothing had been altered since he left seven months ago.

"You know, same old…still getting paid twice per month," Dave said with a fake smile.

It was this downtrodden attitude germane to those at his work, which made Isaac depressed at times. Rather than being grateful that they had good benefits, job security and a living wage, public sector workers always felt "wronged." It seemed endemic, especially as it was figuratively cudgeled into you over and over by the media and your colleagues that you were overworked and underpaid, when in fact you were often underworked, and in the cases of many veteran state employees, overpaid.

Dave continued with his acerbic tone and pabulum until he got to an important point: some budget cuts were made to the museum, and though no one had been laid off, raises were being frozen, which, most importantly, included *promotions and re-classifications!* Dave projected the blame on "greedy Republicans," even though 95% of New York City was Democrat-controlled.

Isaac didn't often check the local government news out of New York City while in Knoxville, but he also figured there was a decent chance someone from work --- office manager, executive director, etc – might have told him this news, since he was spending an entire year away from his family in order to achieve a reclassification and raise.

Isaac knew no one was "going to bat for him" either. And further, he realized the intransigence of the state budget people, so that was basically that.

"Dave, when did this happen?" Isaac asked.

"The decision was made unilaterally a few weeks ago," Dave said, pretending to look at something on his monitor.

"Ok, and could someone have told me?" Isaac asked with a hint of anger.

"I don't know," Dave answered. "You know that we cannot afford our opinion."

It was a cliché Dave used often, and though regularly accurate, made no sense in this instance. Isaac was livid, and Dave was more concerned with himself and surely not Isaac's plight. He imagined Dave – single, no children, with a rent-controlled apartment two subway stops away – in Isaac's precarious familial situation, and how apoplectic he'd be in comparison. When gas prices went up or the "big business" made money, Dave was miffed and envious, but here he seemed apathetic since the misfortune was not his.

Isaac told Dave he was going up to the office to talk with the managers there and he'd be back later – even though he knew that was untrue. Dave nodded and said, halfheartedly, "Good seeing you, Isaac."

Isaac felt as uncomfortable and unimportant in the administrative office as he did downstairs, and the answers were confirmed. Unless he was terribly mistaken or wanted to appeal, he was getting his Masters at the University of Tennessee for no immediate reason other than pride. Any reclassification was not going to occur for more than a year. Isaac was miffed by his own naiveté. He felt this sneaky move by the powers-that-be served as a confirmation of his own lack of realism about people's motivations and intentions. This was beyond odious, but Isaac was a self-reliant individual who abhorred blaming others. He departed, searched for a quick bite to eat, and a walk through Central Park to clear his head and ponder this new and unexpected dilemma.

The most "radical" decision would be to quit. But was that such a stretch now? Isaac certainly was unconcerned with besmirching his reputation at work or in the world of New York City museums. It almost seemed as though, considering Ana's job situation, and now his, as well as his time in Knoxville yet complete, that G-d was sending Isaac Hyde a sign: "Move On." Certainly. It was undeniable that recent events were inimical to any future stability for the Hyde family in New York or New Jersey.

Perhaps this message began when Isaac chose to leave the northeast for his Masters seven months ago, and the circle was now completing itself. Doesn't everything happen for a reason? All these thoughts ruminated through Isaac's head at such an intense pace that he did not notice he was wearing only a light sweater on a 50 degree windy day in Manhattan. He had not planned to be outside this long, but this exegesis of his current state was imperative right now. This was his moment.

Isaac did not mention to Ana what had occurred in Manhattan until the night before he left. This was probably bad timing, since he sought to avoid any arguments upon departure, but he also did not want to interrupt his time with the family while he was visiting.

Isaac knew Ana left in little over a fortnight for her Indiana interview, so he figured sooner was better. They went out alone for dinner the Saturday night before he was to head back to Knoxville, assuming he went at all.

"Dear, I want to finish the program down there," Isaac proudly told Ana.

"Isaac, I know you do, and plan to…," Ana said.

"What if I finished it and there was no reward for all the hard work?" he asked.

Ana looked up from her chicken marsala at their favorite local restaurant with a confused look.

Isaac hated to "sully" the meal with such serious and potentially divisive chatter, but he had no choice.

"Isaac, define "no reward," she asked. "I have no idea on earth what that means."

Isaac explained at length about what happened earlier in the week when he visited the office, as well as the budget issues, how they related to his job and her new possibilities in Indiana. He also mentioned the downtrodden mentality there as compared to campus life. It was a bad comparison, but Ana seemed to appreciate it. Isaac closed by confidently saying he still planned to finish the final few weeks in Tennessee to obtain the Masters degree, "which will better set us up for the future."

Ana, often incurably optimistic, seemed to understand.

"Look, Isaac, I think it's admirable, and I hope it winds up being worth it," she admitted.

Knowing Ana's private sector job would pay more money that his, and simply based on her profession, she'd likely find work quicker whenever and wherever they moved, Isaac did not want to seem otiose. Moreover, he was 80% done with his school year.

Ana was concerned about the time frame, in terms of who'd take care of the kids when she went for the interview and if she had to begin her job – assuming she was in fact hired – before Isaac returned home the second week of May.

Isaac gave the cliché "cross that bridge when we come to it" answer, but he really meant it. They had no idea if and when Ana would be hired, so it was not worth worrying about every detail now. After some coaxing from Isaac, Ana agreed.

Isaac left for Knoxville the next morning. Ana would be with the children for another few weeks until her job officially laid her off, and she went for her interview. They had a family friend in college who would look after Lauren and Ross as best she could while their mom was away.

27

Isaac returned to spring time in Knoxville. Actually, for the first few days, it felt like summer, with late March temps pushing close to 80 before those highs "cooled" back to the mid 60s. With the improved weather, and finals more than a month away, everything seemed calm and happy around town and campus – a bitter contrast to much of Isaac's "vacation" week in the New York area. Nonetheless, upon Ana's recommendation, Isaac tried to relax and enjoy himself. He attended some local baseball games -- the minor league's Tennessee Smokies and the University of Tennessee's team -- and truly had a good few weeks. He chose not to contact Becky, who he presumed was okay, and who also was probably unsure if Isaac had even returned.

On April 7, Ana departed for the Circle City of Indianapolis, Indiana. The kids seemed content with their caretaker, Rachel, a friend of the family and a senior at Rutgers University. Though Rachel was a pretty 22 year old who they knew enjoyed going out and having fun, the Hydes had used her services before, and were certain she'd not allow Lauren to do anything she should not.

Ana called Isaac in Knoxville from her parents when she arrived in Indiana. Isaac was out preparing for some presentations that came around in a few weeks and was not in the mood to talk. Additionally, there really was no need to, aside from confirming that Ana had arrived in the Heartland safely, that her parents were healthy, and that Rachel was doing okay in her first few hours with the kids. Isaac said as much to Ana, and she agreed. They said good night. It was that simple, especially since she had an interview the next morning at 10:30am.

Isaac awoke the next morning to a dark sky with intermittent showers. He also felt bad about being short with Ana last night and felt the need to call her, apologize, and be more upbeat since she was going in for an interview that would direct the next few years of their life.

But when he called her cell phone, it was a tad after ten, and Ana was in transit, with her parents, over to Carmel for the interview, and just couldn't talk at length. That was okay with Isaac. Just hearing her strong voice and knowing she was gung-ho about the potential job in Indiana put his mind at ease.

That was important with Ana Mendez-Hyde, as when she became angst-ridden, it could last that way for awhile. Going into an interview, an energetic, upbeat mindset was essential for her, especially as this was her first job interview in nearly two decades. Isaac knew the same situation would arise for him in the coming year as the family hit this crossroads and he searched for work in wherever his new home might be.

Isaac spent the next few hours picturing Ana in the interview, pondering the prospects of her being accepted for this position, and the decisions and adjustments that would come afterwards. For one thing, he knew Ana would make a good presentation. Far from obsequious, she was usually business-like, unruffable, carrying herself skillfully.

Just as he was sitting down for lunch, the phone rang. It was Ana. She sounded enthusiastic, so right there, Isaac knew the answer: she had not technically been hired, but Ana was rather perspicacious, and was certain she was going to be given the job in the next day or two after some "other interviews," which she sensed were mere formalities to her "coronation."

"Isaac, I am very qualified, and I could tell they were impressed, especially with a Hoosier girl desiring to bring her skills back home," she piped. "My Spanish skills are also an attractive asset."

The next day, Ana called to say she was officially hired. She was asked to begin on April 19, just a little over a week later. This caused a predicament, since even if Isaac was granted permission to take his final exams and give his presentations and papers early, he could be home no earlier than his birthday, May 9. That left nearly three long weeks in between, so Ana asked to begin after May. She was luckily granted May 10, the Monday after Isaac returned. They'd have a day together prior: Isaac's 47th birthday. It was perfect.

28

But sometimes the best laid plans don't always work out perfectly. Not that all went awry, but Rachel turned out to be a bit more feral that they'd like, and Lauren, who had matured quite a bit since her Knoxville trip, reverted back to some bad habits. When Ana returned from Indiana, Lauren was obnoxious; Ross was quiet and distant. Worse, the Hydes had to officially tell the children they'd be moving and leaving their friends in the coming weeks. No hint as to the outcome of Ana's interview had even been given to this point. Mom would depart in a few weeks, after the big birthday bash in early May, then Isaac would "play dad" for a little over a month until school ended and the full move was implemented. That sounded easy. The end of the school year seemed ideal for a move, as did the ages of the children.

Much like military strategy, this was easier conceived and analyzed than implemented. Ross was beginning middle school next fall, and Lauren, though just finishing her first year at high school, was popular and connected to many friends and organizations. She would not be an easy one to conciliate, but in reality, she was 15 and therefore had no choice.

Back in Knoxville, the dog days of April rolled along and it seemed that the mercury rose a few degrees every hour. It was not as scorching as when Isaac arrived in late August, but with his air conditioner on the fritz, and doing a little packing and cleaning each day, the days were long and tiring.

Isaac fielded calls from Ana nightly. She was done working now, having been "let go" from her job in mid-April. Therefore, Ana was tending to the children and moving situation constantly, which seemed like more work than actually having a 40 hour per week job, she often noted to Isaac. He understood, or at least he told her he did. But as of the final week of April, with Isaac in lockdown mode trying to finish papers and study for his exams so as to have that elusive Masters degree in hand (or writing) when he hit the road back on May 9, Ana had yet to tell the children of their upcoming relocation. In fact, she had not even given them a hint, aside from a few scattered boxes around the house that the oblivious children apparently hadn't noticed.

One night, Ana called Isaac and asked if it was a good time to talk.

"Isaac, we need to tell them about the move," she said.

"Ok, let's do this together," he agreed.

Isaac chucked to himself, realizing Ana would bear the personal "brunt" of the kids' reaction either way.

Lauren and Ross gathered by their mom and the phone.

"Kids, your dad and I have an important announcement," said Ana.

"You're pregnant… or getting divorced?" Lauren yelled with a cynical smile toward Ross, who laughed nervously.

Ana gave her a serious look and said "no, neither."

Isaac piped in over the speakerphone, "Look, this is serious and it'll affect both of you also."

Suddenly the children, whose favorite topic was usually themselves, were attentive.

Being over phone and thus out of sight, Isaac had a few notes in front of him in terms of how to approach this subject, since he and Ana, perhaps wrongly, had only given the kids a slight clue about the move up to now. But Isaac realized a turgid explanation would not register with the kids, once the bottom line was explained. So he just went right into it:

"As you know, mom lost her job," he said. "There's good news, though."

There was silence on the phone, which was important.

"She's been hired – by a company in Indiana."

Still silence. Isaac wondered what the faces of his kids looked like back in New Jersey with Ana.

"So, we're going to be moving there once school's done in June," he stated with a slight intonation in his voice, hoping for a good reaction.

More silence.

Finally, Ana spoke.

"Is that okay guys?" she asked. "The timing is good, no?"

Lauren, of course, asked if she and Ross "got a say" in this, and Ana explained that adults make decisions and she was sorry for not letting them know sooner, but there was still nearly two months until the move.

Lauren sulked, but deep inside, Ana knew her daughter understood. Ross was quiet, as usual. He'd be open to it, especially since he liked Indiana's open spaces, and the state's prideful, friendly folks. Lauren, a popinjay like many her age, would miss the malls, materialism and "culture" of the tri-state area, but she'd survive. She'd easily make new friends, male and female. That's just how she was.

Isaac hung up the phone that night, pleased. And even though he knew Ana would receive the complaints and questions, he truly felt she'd handle it well, and that more importantly, the kids were not that upset. Surprised? Maybe, but they did not seem angry overall. Isaac counted his blessings that night – for his wife, his family and his life past, present and future.

Conclusion

Isaac breezed through finals a week later, finished up some quality papers and his presentations were a formality to the nearly perfect grades he attained for the spring semester.

He was on his way home.

The sky looked bluer than usual when Isaac prepared to depart eastern Tennessee for the final time. The temperature was a perfect 74 degrees at 8:30am on May 9, his birthday. The air was fresh and the mountains beckoned for Isaac to push through them one final time. As he moved north, Isaac felt the still-cool May wind whipping through the open windows. He'd definitely miss the community, the "feel" and other aspects of Appalachia and the upper south – but he was now opening a new and exciting chapter of his life. He was going "home," but only briefly. New Jersey's chapter was closing concurrently with Tennessee's; Indiana was next.

Life was short. Living and dying in a four-mile radius was never Isaac Hyde's goal. This would never be the case now, in any possible way. Ana's warm heart, talented mind and his kids' love would be waiting around the next bend of life. And for that, Isaac Hyde realized his year in this "Marble City" was more than worthwhile; it was a necessary blessing.

Worldly Acknowledgements

This book, which as anyone who knows me and Maria realizes is somewhat of a work of "realistic fiction," was an arduous task. It was my third published book, but the first of the fictional variety. For years, friends and family had cajoled me to write something other than non-fiction. It was not easy, mostly because I rarely read or watch fiction. It's not that I don't have an imagination, but to me, life is short, yet enthralling, and I like to think deeply about it at all times. Fantasies don't appeal to me, since I need to reserve my time for what matters: my family, friends, work, travel, religion, et al. That's why this book seemed a compromise, loosely based on the realities of my life and others, but surely a tale. Including cities, sites and themes that were reality-based made the book much easier to write. I hope others will enjoy the words within.

Though this was not a research book requiring too much guidance, I wanted to still make some necessary thank yous:

Maria, my love, you continue to amaze me each day with your compassion, kind heart, bravery and sincerity. The topics and stories in this book are a tribute to us, especially since you helped me with your psychological expertise and intriguing tidbits from your imagination. Thank you for all you are to me. I cannot wait to spend my life with you.

And to mom and dad, it bears repeating that, without you, there is no Ari. I am overjoyed that you are my parents and a major part of my life. Ron, as a stepfather, your positive influence during my formative years was necessary for my growth as a human.

To my friends and acquaintances who still seek guidance from me, but also bequeath their own, solicited or unsolicited, I am forever indebted.

To America's Silent Victors: My mission and passion ad infinitum. Without your noble efforts, we'd be speaking a different language, enjoying less freedom and fewer opportunities. Most of us do, in fact, realize the sacrifices you make for our country.

And lastly, to G-d, without you, *nothing is possible*. That special plan you have in store for all of us is what makes life worthwhile. I hope more people understand the personal relationship you have with each and every one of your creations, big and small.

Ari J. Kaufman
www.ajkauf.com
Friendswood, IN.
October 18, 2009